TRAGEDY ON THE BARLOW ROAD

A WESTERN FRONTIER ADVENTURE

ROBERT PEECHER

For information the author may be contacted at PO Box 967; Watkinsville GA; 30677

or at rob@mooncalfpress.com

This is a work of fiction. Any similarities to actual events in whole or in part are purely accidental. None of the characters or events depicted in this novel are intended to represent actual people.

ISBN – 9798863805801

CONTENTS

1

Towser's bark broke harsh in the hollow silence of the snow covered mountain.

Everything gray except the black and white dog, now more white than usual with the accumulation of snow on his coat. The clouds hung like a fog on the mountain, the branches on the great, tall fir trees and ponderosa pines seemed to hug their trunks under the weight of the snow that clung to the needles. Even the splashes of autumn color among the evergreens were dulled by the low clouds hanging among the trees.

The gray clouds, wet all around them, the snow hanging from the trees above, piled perhaps three or four inches deep on the bare spaces, but deep enough that it obscured the trail.

Zeke Townes hugged himself as he looked through the trees, trying to see what had stirred Towser's ire.

"It's all right, boy," Zeke said, bending slightly to give the dog a pat on the shoulder.

He did not know that it was all right. They'd encountered some Indians down in the valley before making the push up into the Blue Mountains. That had been six days ago. The Natives had come down out of the mountains with sacks of pine nuts they'd gathered for the winter. Language had presented some troubles. Someone among the emigrants decided the

1

Indians must be Paiutes, and no one had any reason to object. Through broken English – and only a few words of that – and hand gestures that might have meant anything, Zeke, his brother Elias, and some of the other men in the wagon train who tried to communicate with the Paiutes all had the sense that the Indians were warning the emigrants away from the mountains.

Could they have known this storm was coming?

Zeke thought maybe so. Maybe the Natives who'd been in this Northwest Territory for a thousand years or more could perhaps read Nature's signs and predict a coming storm.

"What's he barking at?" Marie asked, coming out of the tent.

"Probably just some snow falling from a branch," Zeke said.

They'd heard the branches snapping under the weight of the ice and snow all through the morning, a sudden snapping and crashing, muffled and hollow like every other noise, like they had driven their livestock and wagons right into some enormous tin pot packed with snow and pine needles where every sound came roaring and softened at the same time.

"You should go back into the tent. Try to stay warm," Zeke said.

"It's very tranquil here," Marie said. "Like a dream."

A nightmare, Zeke thought.

For five hundred miles or more, every man in the wagon train feared two things, river crossings and snow in the Blue Mountains.

A thousand delays haunted them.

They'd arrived late to St. Joseph and found no wagon train captains available to them – at least, none they would trust. They hired a boy who'd been once with some trappers as far as Jim Bridger's trading post. He said he could guide them that far, and he'd done the job well enough.

They'd had stampeded cattle. Broken wheels. High water.

At Bridger's they'd hired new guides, seven men who turned out to be downright rascals. Worse than that. Scoundrels of the more horrible kind. Those men led them on a "southern route" that did not exist. They promised it would mean the Townes Party could avoid crossing the Snake River, but they'd misled the emigrants about how bad the conditions would be. And then those men abandoned them, trying to steal women when they left. It had meant even more delay as they chased the bandits into some mountains to recover the women and stolen money.

Finally, the Townes Party rejoined the beaten path of the Oregon Trail near Fort Boise.

Dangerously low on supplies, they crafted a raft so that a few of them could cross the Snake River with the hopes of buying supplies at the fort. But they found the fort all but abandoned. Only native tribes occupied the fort. They were friendly enough, and had some English and French from the French-Canadians who occupied the fort. But they had only some potatoes and salmon that they would sell.

Then came three days of hard rain, and the Malheur River jumped its banks. What should have been an easy river crossing turned into almost a week lost as they waited for the rains to subside and the river to drop out.

They fought through a rugged countryside, dry as a bone, before finally coming into a long valley with the Blue Mountains looming ominously over their left shoulders and the equally imposing Wallowas on their right shoulders.

But for Zeke Townes and his brother Elias, the tree covered mountains gave them great hope.

They'd come more than fifteen hundred miles now, bringing their families and several hired men, with the expectation of building a sawmill and working a timber lease. They'd been promised by the man who sold it to

3

them that they'd find trees that reached into the sky, as tall and straight as they could imagine. But through the majority of those fifteen hundred miles they'd covered, there wasn't a tree in sight. Both brothers had begun to worry they'd left their homes in Paducah for the promise of a treeless timber lease. But in this valley, they could look left and right and see more trees than a thousand men could cut in two lifetimes.

The ever-present fear, though, as they lost days to sudden stampedes, sickness, and the ceaseless array of calamities that could befall a wagon train, was now on them. Literally, falling from the sky all around them. Snow in the Blue Mountains.

Had they come this far only to be stranded?

"You should go back into the tent," Zeke said again to his wife.

She had a wool blanket around her shoulders that she hugged closer to her now.

"I'm all right, Zeke," she said with a smile. "It's not so cold."

Zeke scoffed.

"It's cold enough."

He had only his vest and suit coat. The necessity of keeping the load light, Zeke brought nothing heavier than the suit coat. The wind cut through him and he shivered.

Marie walked to him, opening her arms with the blanket covering them, and she wrapped her arms around him, giving him a moment's relief against the cold.

"Perhaps you're the one who should go into the tent," she suggested.

More than thirty wagons snaked along the narrow path winding between the trees standing like thousands of centurions on the hillsides either side of them. Towering and strong. Keeping a silent vigil. Watching over the path where the wagons passed.

Marie's dark hair catching the flakes of snow. Her hazel eyes moving over Zeke's face. Bearded, now. Burnt by the sun.

The yellow dog, they called that one Mustard, he came out of the tent now, bounding through the snow. Towser chased after him and the two of them went barking into the blackness of the forest.

"I should go in and check on Daniel," Marie said after several moments standing with her arms around her husband. "Shall I leave the blanket with you?"

"No. I'll be all right. You keep it and stay warm."

Marie nodded. But she didn't move away yet.

"Will we be able to get through?" she asked.

The snow had started the previous afternoon. Elias, who was elected captain of the wagon train shortly after they crossed the Missouri River all the way back near St. Jo, he'd called a stop for the day. They did not know how much worse the snow might be up higher on the mountain, and already the road was beginning to ice. The wagons sat where they were. The men rounded up the livestock and took them back about half a mile to a wide meadow covered in grass. By dark, only a little snow had fallen. Most of the snow came down overnight while they slept, though it was no great surprise to Zeke when he emerged from his tent and found the canvas covering the wagons, the road, the trees, and the tents all covered in snow. In the woods, most of the ground was still bare. The snow had fallen as far as the thick branches and come no farther. But clear spots were covered in snow, and patches of it here and there had found a way through the canopy.

"As long as it's no worse up higher, I think we can get through," Zeke said.

"What will happen if it is worse up higher?" Marie asked.

"We might be stranded for a few days."

She nodded her head, thinking about what that would mean.

"Days, or months?"

"It won't be months," Zeke said quickly. "This is the first snow of the season. It will melt. We'll have a muddy slog getting up and over the mountains, but we won't be stranded."

Daniel, their young son, made a noise inside the tent. Marie shut her eyes and tossed her head that way. Zeke nodded.

"I'll talk to Elias and come back to let you know something."

THE SNOW CRUNCHED UNDER Elias's feet as he walked along the wagon train.

Up and down the path, emigrants were emerging from their tents or out of their wagons. They stretched out the knots from the hard ground or the cramped quarters of the wagon bed. And they marveled at the overnight snowfall.

Some of the children, oblivious to the dangers the snow represented, began to run and laugh and play in the stuff.

"What will this mean for the day?" a woman asked as Elias passed by.

"I'm not certain yet, ma'am," Elias said.

Wiser McKinney walked a ways with Elias as he passed by the two wagons belonging to the McKinney brothers.

"Good morning, Mr. Townes."

"I hope it is, Mr. McKinney," Elias said dryly.

"What does the snow mean for our ability to continue moving forward?" Wiser asked.

Elias took a heavy breath. He did not know the answer, and he certainly did not want to start panicked rumors among the emigrants. Snow meant death. Snow meant disaster. Snow meant they'd lost the trail. They could manage it here, probably, but on narrow ledges with steep drops, they'd be risking the loss of life and property.

"I don't know exactly, Mr. McKinney," Elias said. "But it would be good if the snow would stop falling."

The next wagon belonged to Sophie Bloom. Her stomach now noticeably larger. Pregnant and with three children, already, and now a husband buried back along the banks of the Bear River. With the loss of her husband, Cody Page had taken over driving her wagon. Cody was one of the hired men headed west with the Townes brothers to start a sawmill and timber business. Cody had worked for Elias and Zeke back in Paducah. His brother Will had come along as well and was now back with the cow column, managing the livestock.

Elias had not picked Cody by accident to be Sophie Bloom's driver. Though she already had three children, with the fourth on the way, Sophie Bloom was still a young woman. About Cody's age. And she was now bound for Oregon Territory with no husband and no prospects. Cody, of all his hired men who were still single, was mature. Sturdy. He'd make a good husband to any woman. He was the sort, too, who would look after children even if they weren't his own.

Now Cody lifted one of Sophie Bloom's young boys from the back of the wagon and set him on his feet in the snow. Cody tousled the boy's hair and sent him off to play before lifting out the next child.

Cody caught sight of Elias and a worried look passed between the two men.

"I think it's snowing harder than it was just a minute ago," Elias said.

Cody chewed his lip.

"I'm going to get Mrs. Bloom settled here, and then walk back to check on the boys. Anything you want me to tell them?"

"Send Henry Blair up here," Elias said.

What Cody referred to as "the boys," those were the other hired hands and a couple of packers who drove the livestock. Henry Blair was the closest thing to a guide the Townes Party had. When they left out of St. Joseph, there'd been no wagon train captains to hire – at least, none that Elias was willing to hire. Those who remained in the city so late in the season were drunks or cheats or both. But he'd found Henry Blair. Though still a young man, Henry had been as far west as Bridger's Fort when he'd come out with a group of trappers. He'd agreed to come along as a guide for the Townes Party, though he'd refused to take on the role of captain. And he'd been adamant that once they reached Bridger's Fort, he'd be useless to them as anything more than a hired hand.

But Elias had found Henry to be better than that. He had a knack for reading terrain. He'd spent a winter at Bridger's which gave him insight that certainly none of the others had. Maybe he'd not been this far west, but he'd hunted and trapped in a Northwest Territory winter, and that made him invaluable.

"I'll send Henry up," Cody said.

Beyond Sophie Bloom's wagon, Elias came to John Gordon. He and his wife Beth had just come out of their wagon. The two of them stood together, huddled under a blanket.

"Mr. Townes!" John Gordon called as Elias passed by.

"Good morning, Mr. Gordon," Elias said curtly, hoping to pass by without conversation.

"What does this snow mean?" John Gordon persisted.

"It means we'll probably be here for a day or two," Elias said.

"You do not intend to push forward?"

"I haven't made up my mind," Elias told him. "For now, we should all behave as if we'll be rolling out of here in a couple of hours. Prepare your breakfast, be thankful we have firewood. I'll know better within the hour what my intentions are."

"Mr. Townes," Beth Gordon said, abandoning the blanket with her husband and walking directly up to Elias. "Please tell me if I am wrong, but it is my understanding that snow could prove disastrous to a wagon party."

"It could, ma'am," Elias said with a sigh. "But this ain't much snow, so I'm hoping it won't cause much disaster, neither. If it lets up in the next couple of hours, it will only delay us some."

"And if it persists? Or gets worse?"

Elias nodded his head helplessly.

"If it persists, it might delay us for a day or two. If it gets worse, we might have to think about going back down into the valley we come out of."

"Turning around?"

Elias nodded his head.

"That might be an option, Mrs. Gordon, but we don't know that yet. I would greatly appreciate it if you wouldn't say anything that would alarm the others."

The request was made in futility, Elias knew. Beth Gordon had proved herself to be a terrible gossip. She crowded around in the evenings with many of the other women in the wagon train to spread whatever rumors she had heard or conjured in her mind. Elias knew it would be only a matter of minutes before she found someone to complain to that they might have to turn around. But just now, he didn't care too much what rumors spread through the wagon train. Now he had greater concerns than rumors.

He had no idea what to expect from a snow storm this early in the season in the Blue Mountains. Could it turn into a blizzard?

A foot of snow, Elias would feel confident pushing through. They could reach the summit and work their way down the west side of the mountain. Even if it took them two weeks to make the fifty miles or so it would take to clear the mountains, they could get through in a foot of snow.

But a blizzard? Four feet of snow, or five? They'd never make it. And as they neared the summit, they must expect that the snow would be deeper.

If they were back home in Kentucky and the first snow of the year fell, it wouldn't even be a thought in his mind. In two days, or three, the snow would all be gone. Might it be the same here?

"Mr. Townes, may I have a moment?"

He'd broken free of Beth Gordon, but now – at the very next wagon – he encountered Jeb Smith and his father, Hezekiah.

"Mr. Smith," Elias said with a nod at Jeb and another at his father.

"We're understandably concerned, Mr. Townes," Jeb Smith said. "We've encountered one disaster followed by another, and we're facing snow in the mountains. I don't think I need to tell you just how dire a predicament we're in."

Elias nodded his head.

"I think it remains to be seen if it is a dire predicament, Mr. Smith," Elias said. "It's not so much snow, just yet."

"Those guides you hired that took us south of the Snake River. The rains that delayed us. Snow, now."

"Yes, Mr. Smith. We haven't had our troubles to seek."

The Smiths were one of the families who joined the Townes Party back at Bridger's Fort. They'd come that far with a wagon train bound for California, but intending to go on to Oregon Territory instead, the Smiths and a couple of other families had joined up with the Townes Party. They'd been decent folks, all of them, and whatever complaints they might have had about their new traveling companions, they'd kept to themselves.

"We have grave concerns, Mr. Townes," Jeb Smith said. "It seems impossible that we will reach Oregon City this year. And we're wondering now if we wouldn't be better off turning back into the valley from which we've just come."

"Winter in the valley?" Elias frowned at the man.

"That's the thinking my father and I share," Jeb Smith said with a nod to Hezekiah.

Elias figured Hezekiah to be approaching sixty-years and Jeb not too far from forty. Jeb had with him also his wife and two sons. The boys were both teenagers. Both of them fit and able, if a little young.

"As a group, I believe we could get through the winter in pretty good shape. We have beef on the hoof, dairy cows, and plenty of guns and ammunition both for hunting and defense. That river running through the valley has fish in it, and I believe we could forage for edible plants."

"I've noticed bittercress and chickweed," Hezekiah cut in. "Dandelion roots that we can roast as coffee. Many other edible plants. And I'm confident that the local natives would be willing to trade with us."

Elias frowned.

"Maybe not," he said. "I expect they'll have just what they need to get themselves through the winter."

"Even so, we can ration our flour and beans and rice. If we all pitch in together," Hezekiah said.

Jeb Smith cut in.

"We have men enough to protect a small community, and time that we can build shelters to see us through the winter."

Elias heaved a sigh.

"I'll certainly consider what you've said. I do not now think the road is impassable. If we can clear the Blue Mountains, there are mission settlements that we can reach. Perhaps it's too late to get to Oregon City, but we should still be able to get to the settlements this side of the Columbia River."

Jeb Smith dropped his shoulders. He seemed bitterly disappointed, but he accepted Elias's answer.

As he continued along the line of wagons, it was more of the same. Every man who emerged from his tent or wagon seemed eager to offer Elias some piece of advice or to express a worry. Some thought the wagon train should be moving already and asked after the delay. Others, like the Smiths, wanted to turn back for the valley.

At last, Elias reached his destination. The last wagon in the train. The one that belonged to his younger brother, Ezekiel. He found Zeke standing back down the trail some, at the edge of a stream that ran along beside the trail.

"It would be beautiful if it wasn't such a thorn in my side," Elias said.

The snow rested at the top of rocks protruding from the stream bed, all along its banks. Brown and black, gray and bright white. Crystal clear water. Elias had an urge to dip a cup straight into the spring. He wondered if he'd ever seen water so pure.

"Thorn or not, it's a pretty view."

The big pines rose up on the other side of the stream, but down below them there was just enough of a break in the contour of the land that through the tree tops they could see south to the high snow-covered peaks.

"Yes, thorn or not," Elias conceded.

"We're lucky to be able to see this, brother. In the great scale of things, not many Anglos have or ever will see such sights as we've seen."

"It's an arduous journey," Elias said. "But in years to come, they'll tame it. They'll stretch tracks across this whole countryside."

Zeke nodded his head.

"Maybe so. But not in our lifetimes. It's too wild out here in this west. It'll take a hundred years or more to get trains this far."

Elias took in the view a moment longer. Looking at the distant snow-capped peaks in silence gave him a reprieve from having to consider what he'd come to talk about. But the necessity of action forced him to speech.

"Some folks think we should turn back. Spend winter in the valley. Finish our journey in the spring."

Zeke clicked his tongue.

"You think the snow will get worse?" Zeke asked.

"I don't know," Elias said. "But if it does get worse, we don't want to be trapped on this mountain."

"Uh-huh. And we know it'll be bad up higher."

"This could turn very quickly on us," Elias said. "If we're on the front side of a blizzard, we could have four or five feet of snow in a couple of days. We could easily find ourselves stranded."

"What do you think about turning back?" Zeke asked.

"I think it's a bad choice, but better than being stuck here."

"I'm for moving forward," Zeke said. "Even if we have to go slow."

"I don't want to lose the trail," Elias said. "Even as it is now, I could see us wandering off the path. Deeper into the mountains. We'd never come out."

Zeke took a heavy breath.

"Send riders ahead to scout out the situation up higher. Can we reach the summit? Can we keep to the trail? See where things are in the morning. If the snow gets worse and the trail is impassable up above us, we turn these wagons and make for the valley in the morning."

"That's my thinking."

"I don't like the idea of going back, even if it's just into the valley," Zeke said. "I set out for Oregon City, and that's where I intend to go."

"I agree," Elias said. "But better to arrive there in the summer than starve to death on this mountainside."

"You think we could survive the winter?" Zeke asked.

"Down in the valley? Sure. So long as we don't lose the livestock."

Zeke nodded. Every decision could prove fatal, but that was nothing new. It had been that way since they'd crossed the Missouri River. But this wasn't just a decision to cross a river or take a cutoff. This was a decision with a months-long implication.

"I suppose I'm one of the riders you want to send forward?" Zeke asked.

"I thought you and Henry Blair would be the two best to send."

2

THE MOUNTAIN FOREST WAS so quiet, Zeke could hear every breath the big gray horse took. Each time a hoof crunched snow and broke ice. When a clump of snow fell from a high tree top to splash on the ground below.

Everything else was all silence.

"It's hard to believe the whole entire world ain't peaceful like this," Henry Blair said, speaking hardly above a whisper.

"It's hard to think of this as peaceful," Zeke said.

"Why do you say that?" Henry asked.

"If we get stuck in this snow, Henry, a fair few of us won't be coming off this mountain."

The trail followed the natural contour of the land, winding around a long spur coming down from the heights above, up through a draw and along a ridge. For the first couple of miles, the trail was easy enough to follow even though it was covered in snow. It kept near to a creek and cut a wide swath between the pines. They picked their way through the snow. The higher they climbed, the more the low clouds hanging over the mountain prevented them from seeing much ahead. They had no concept of how high up the mountain they'd come or how much higher the mountain might go.

The two riders came into a wide and long clearing. Not only had the fog grown thicker, but here, especially, the snow was much deeper. The horses had to high step to walk through the stuff.

"Can we get the wagons through this?" Henry asked.

Zeke gave a small shake to his head and frowned as he looked around.

"Everything depends on what this storm does," Zeke said. "If it blows over and the sun comes out, we'll be clear of these mountains in less than a week."

"And if it opens up and dumps more snow on us?" Henry answered his own question: "Stranded."

They moved through the clearing and looked for the trail at the far end. The snow was falling again. Lazily, but steady adding to what was already on the ground.

"We could abandon the wagons," Zeke said. "Pack through the snow and get out of the mountains."

"People ain't gonna like that solution, Mr. Zeke. They've held their possessions mighty dear for a long ways."

"No. They won't care for it at all," Zeke agreed, thinking of the treasured items almost every family in the wagon train had already abandoned at some stage of their journey. "But it's better to get out of here with your life and nothing else than to freeze to death with everything you own."

They followed the trail out a ways farther and found themselves soon at the precipice of a deep canyon. The getting down would be hell with the wagons. The trail dropped at a steep decline into the valley.

"It'll mean ropes and chains here," Henry observed.

"But the snow ain't so bad down in the canyon," Zeke said.

They could not see far into the canyon to know what the trail looked like beyond.

"If it follows the canyon, that'll be easier going once we're down there," Henry said. "But if it goes back up the other side, it could be worse than hell trying to get out of there."

Zeke started to laugh, and Henry glanced at him as if he'd lost his mind. Zeke wondered if maybe Henry was right, if maybe he had lost his mind. The cold bit at Zeke's face. His fingers were numb on the horse's reins. He wore a pair of leather work gloves, but they were made for swinging an ax in all sorts of weather, not to keep his hands warm. His coat was insufficient to keep out the breeze.

"This cold weather came too early," Zeke said.

"Yes, sir. And we came too late."

"What do you think, Henry? If I told you to go back and report to Elias and tell him what to do, what would you say to him?"

"I'd say push on through and make certain every man in the wagon train is a praying Christian. That's what I'd tell him."

Zeke laughed again.

"All right, then. Let's go see how many Christians we've got in the wagon train."

They wheeled the horses and turned back. Deliberately riding outside the tracks they'd left on the way out so as to tamp down more of the snow. They kept their thoughts to themselves, though both men knew what the other was thinking – or near enough – because their thoughts so closely mirrored each other.

A thousand things could go wrong. More snow. A blizzard. The temperatures could drop. Frostbite could become a worry. The livestock could start to drop. Or maybe the sun would come out, warm things up, turn all this snow into water, and the trail might become a bog of mud, sucking the wagon wheels into the morass. The solution to one problem might only lead to a worse problem.

It was nearing dark when Henry and Zeke could hear the sounds coming up the trail from the wagon train. Children laughing. The McKinney brothers had their guitars out and were playing a tune. Cattle lowing. A dog barking. Zeke recognized the bark. Someone was throwing a stick for Towser. And there was Mustard, with his deeper bark. Towser always won the race to the stick and hurried back with it, and Mustard would always give him a deep, surly bark as Towser raced past. Zeke would always toss one right to Mustard to let him feel like he'd done his job.

And then they could smell the campfire smoke, hanging there on the side of the mountain, pressed down by the weight of the clouds.

Then they could see the wagons, the front ones, anyway. The dogs saw them coming first, running at them and barking a warning until they realized it was Zeke, and then their barks turned joyful, a pitch higher. Elias came behind the dogs, a chewed-on pine stick in his hand. Elias never did care for dogs the way Zeke did, and the fact he was entertaining Zeke's dog with a game of fetch was testament to the weight on his shoulders. Any distraction he could find would suffice, even a game of fetch.

The guitars stopped and word spread quickly down the line of wagons that the riders had returned.

Zeke dismounted in front of Elias, and Henry took the gray horse's reins and led Duke back down the line toward the other livestock.

"Well?" Elias said. "What did you find."

Some of the other men were hurrying forward. Smith and Weiss came together. The McKinney brothers didn't even bother to set down their guitars. Zeke noted that they both wore mittens with their fingers exposed so they could play. Others were coming up from farther toward the back, some of them running.

"It won't be easy," Zeke said, weighing his words against the expectations of those gathering around them. "The snow gets thicker, and the trail is difficult. We followed as far as we could reasonably go, and I'd say it's still passable. If we wake to deeper snow, we might want to consider going back. But if we wake in the morning and it's no deeper and there's no sign of the weather turning worse, then I would recommend that we press on."

A cheer went up among some. Others seemed to take it as unwelcome news.

"I'll add, too, that Henry believes we have a better chance if this wagon train is full of praying Christians."

This brought a laugh from the men who cheered and scowls from those who didn't. Zeke would have liked it better if at least a couple of them had fallen on their knees.

3

ELIAS WALKED CLOSE TO the oxen. He gave the one nearest him a vigorous rub on his shoulder.

"Keep them moving, Gabe," he called to his oldest son who drove the team.

It was Solomon McKinney's idea to drive the livestock ahead of the wagons. The thinking was that the horses and cattle would stomp down the snow, clear the path. It had seemed a reasonable idea, and perhaps it had been successful that first day. But the second day, the sun broke through the clouds. The temperature rose enough that Elias was sweating as he walked along. The snow began to melt. Chewed all to hell by the livestock in front of them, the trail turned into a mire. Every step was a fight for the heavy beasts, and a significant distance was growing between the wagons at the front and those at the back.

Caleb Driscoll drove Zeke's wagon, the last in the train, and they were so far back now that Elias wasn't sure if he was leading one wagon train or two or three. In fact, just now, Elias's wagon was a full two hundred yards out in front of the next wagon in the train – this one belonging to the pregnant widow Sophie Bloom. Her husband had been killed when his own wagon struck him going down a steep hill. Elias assigned one of his own hired men, Cody Page, to drive Mrs. Bloom's wagon. But her oxen were struggling now and holding back the entire wagon train. Elias didn't know if it was better to stop and wait for them or to give them a clear path if the beasts caught a second wind.

Lack of water and exhaustion had cost them a fair number of oxen over the last two hundred miles which meant there were fewer oxen to rotate which meant these were more exhausted than the ones they'd lost. Only the heartiest of beasts would survive to see the end of this journey – wherever and whenever that occurred.

In describing what he and Henry had found, Zeke told Elias that they'd gone as far as a deep canyon, but after two days, the wagons had still not reached that canyon. They were three days out now from the morning when Elias sent Zeke and Henry Blair forward to scout. Three days, and they hadn't managed to make it as far as the two riders.

"Pa, maybe we ought to leave the wagons and pack out of the mountains," Gabriel suggested, feeling free to speak his mind as no one was near them. It was a suggestion Gabe had heard passed around the camp in the evenings. Some were for it and some against it, but those for it were only for it if the others would be for it, too. Nobody wanted to abandon all their belongings only to discover in a week's time that their neighbor had come out the other side with wagon and possessions intact.

So none had done it. None had jettisoned their belongings for an easier go of it. But still, at camp in the evenings, it was a constant topic of conversation.

Elias turned to look at his son.

"This wagon, Gabe? If it was nothing but clothes and personals, I'd gladly turn it over right here. Give it to the forest. There's not a thing such as those that can't be replaced. But this wagon? That's got all the tools we need to start our business here in the Northwest Territory. Our axes and saws, our ropes and chains, our nails. I can't abandon those things unless there is no hope of getting them out. If we have to start in Oregon Territory without these tools, we're starting in too deep of a hole. These tools are our livelihood. Every man we hired to come out here with us – Jerry Bennett, the Tucker brothers, the Page brothers, Caleb, your uncle Zeke – these tools are what are going to earn all of those men a living. And if I have to get one wagon through, then I might as well get all of them through."

"Yes, sir," Gabe said, feeling chastised.

"I didn't moan when we lost our possessions and most of our supplies," Elias said, recalling the destruction of his wagon in a failed attempt to float it across the Snake River.

"No, sir."

"I can't lose this wagon, though."

Mountain miles didn't count the same as miles on the prairie. Elias figured they'd done something just under five miles a day the past two days. Today they might be lucky to go three miles.

As Elias turned back around, he saw a rider coming back from the cow column, now in front of the wagons. As he neared, Elias saw it was Will Page, Cody's brother.

"Mr. Townes," Will said. "You might want to saddle up and ride ahead with me."

Elias let out an exasperated breath that he followed with a chuckle and a shake of his head.

"What is it, Will?"

"Mr. Zeke said we'd come to a pretty good descent into a canyon. We've reached it. About two miles up ahead."

Elias couldn't hide the sardonic smile from his face.

"If it's not one thing, it's something else," Elias said.

"Yes, sir," Will said. "I think when you see it for yourself, you're going to agree it's something else."

"That sounds ominous, Mr. Page."

Elias had his palomino, Tuckee, tied to the back of the wagon. His saddle and blanket rode there on the back, so that the horse could be easily saddled. And the wagon was going at such a ponderous pace that there was no need to stop for him to get the horse saddled.

"You might slow down just a little and let the others catch up," Elias told his son as he stepped into the saddle. Then he rode forward with Will Page to see what fresh calamity awaited them.

"IT'S AN EVEN BET if the mud is going to make this hillside so slick you can't control the descent or if it's going to bog everything down and you'll have to push the wagons to get them to roll downhill," Jerry Bennett said, a nasty grin on his face. "Either way, Mr. Townes, I'm glad I'm in charge of the livestock and it ain't my decision to make."

Elias chewed his lip looking over the precipice. Down below, the canyon was wide enough, snow scattered here and there and a little mountain creek running in the bed of the canyon. The horses and cattle were all already down in the canyon, along with several of the men riding in the cow column. The drovers and livestock had made good time when they no longer had the wagons in front of them slowing them down.

"The damn hill looks almost straight down."

Jerry laughed a little.

"Yes, sir. It ain't quite vertical, but it's hard to tell the difference. You should see it from the bottom."

"How'd you manage to get down in the canyon?"

Jerry walked through the snow a ways back down the trail and pointed to a narrow path that cut through the trees.

"It's a switchback trail. Follows a little ridge. Looks like folks before us have used it for livestock, but it's too narrow for a wagon. We had to blanket the heads of some of the horses to get them to go, but my gal Loose went up and down the trail like she was born on the side of a cliff."

Bennett's horse Lucy came from the same mare as Zeke's horse Duke. When they made it out to Oregon City, Jerry Bennett would be the foreman of the crew, and he was the leader among the hired hands now. Five years older than the others, or more, he'd worked for the Townes family for close to twenty years now. He'd started working for Elias's father as a boy and he'd become the number two man at the sawmill back in Paducah. There was nothing Jerry couldn't do. He could build a cabin, cut a tree, drive a column of livestock two thousand miles. He had an easy confidence that Elias sometimes envied.

What differentiated the two of them more than anything was the responsibility. Jerry Bennett didn't have a care in the world. No wife. No children. No wagon train full of pioneers looking to him to make every decision. His only responsibilities were to his wages and with nothing else, a man could always walk away from a job. But Jerry was loyal to the Townes family. But loyalty and responsibility were two different things.

"It can be managed," Jerry said, looking at the expression on Elias's face. "Remove the teams, take them down this switchback trail. Lock the wheels of the wagons. We'll put a team of four oxen on each one, plus a dozen men, and we'll lower the wagons down the hill there. I'm sure it's what the folks before us had to do. Only difference is, we've got ice and mud. And I'm sure plenty of them had mud."

Elias nodded his head.

"We'll be all day getting the wagons down, and probably all day tomorrow."

"Yes, sir. And you better tell them pilgrims to secure their loads. Anything heavy like a stove or a keg of nails is going to bust right through the wagon if it ain't tied in good."

"If you ever have the opportunity to get yourself elected captain of a wagon train, Jerry, I'd advise you to politely decline," Elias said.

Jerry laughed and clapped him on the shoulder.

"Yes, sir, Mr. Townes. You better believe I would decline. Might not even be polite about it. But it's a lucky thing for these pilgrims – most of 'em – that you took on the chore. I don't think most of 'em would've never made it so far without you, Mr. Townes. Think of some of these folks. That Weiss feller that drove off your brother Zeke? That man wouldn't have made it ten miles into Kansas before he had to go back if you hadn't been leading him. Pilcher? He's a decent enough man, but do you think he'd have made it to South Pass? Or them McKinney brothers?"

Elias waved off the praise. He'd not done much, in his mind at least, that anyone else couldn't have done.

"Look here," Elias said, glad for a reason to change the subject. Over near the precipice, he found a couple of stout pine trees where the bark had been skinned away in patches. Elias slid a hand from his glove and ran his hand over the exposed wood. "Smooth. I reckon this is where they tied pulleys to lower the wagons?"

"Uh-huh," Jerry Bennett agreed, running his hand over one of the smooth patches. "What do you guess? Two thousand wagons been lowered down this slope clinging to this tree here?"

"Probably more than that," Elias said.

They waited the better part of an hour before Gabriel finally appeared, leading the first wagon. The trail was narrow through the mountain forest. In many places, wide enough only for one wagon to pass at a time. Here, if they squeezed tight, there might be room enough for three wagons side-by-side, but it appeared earlier emigrants had cut away a fair amount of timber to give themselves room to work.

Elias directed Gabe to stop the wagon well back from the edge of the steep slope. They'd need to have space for at least two or three yokes of oxen to move. The drop was not more than maybe forty feet, but plenty of space for a wagon to get loose, flip, lose its load, or dash itself to bits at the end of a free fall.

"Should I stay up and lend my back?" Jerry Bennett asked.

"Maybe for the first wagon or two," Elias said. "But after that, when the others have seen how the job is done, you should go on back to the livestock and help direct things down below. Get those wagons hitched to teams and out of the way once they're down in the canyon."

With the wagons now stopping behind Gabriel, men were walking forward to see what fresh obstacle they had encountered. There's already been plenty of discussion around campfires about this slope from Zeke's initial report, and that made it worse. The anticipation of this slope had worked on the men, enlivening their imaginations, and now they got their first look at how the real thing would match up to the pictures they'd painted in their minds.

"It's worse than I thought it would be," Wiser McKinney confessed.

Captain Walker, a veteran of the Indian wars in Florida who had already proved himself to be unafraid of the next adventure, had a different view.

"For all the talk about it, I thought it would be much more terrible than it is."

"How are you now, Captain Walker?" Elias called to the man, seeing how red his face had grown as he strained against the weight on the rope.

Walker had stripped down to his undershirt, and still the sweat beaded across his beet forehead. He spluttered a laugh and shook his head at Elias.

"They should mount a sign back at the Missouri River warning that only young men should advance farther," Walker said, breathing gasps in between almost every word. "Let each man decide for himself if he fits the bill."

They'd managed Elias's wagon first down the slope.

With locked wheels and a secured load, they'd employed two teams of men, block and tackle, and two yokes of oxen. Each team of men used a pulley strapped to the wagon and another secured to one of those stout trees, the rope threaded between the pulleys and eight men on each rope lowering the wagon by inches. The oxen were hitched above and walked toward the slope with a couple of men leading the beasts and doing all they could to keep in time with the men on the ropes.

A lot of shouting, a fair amount of arguing, and more than a little cursing, but they got Elias's wagon to the bottom.

Sophie Bloom's went down with the young pregnant widow and her three children holding their breaths as they watched.

The Tucker brothers had a single wagon between them, but it toted the belongings of all the Townes brothers' hired men. The Page brothers, Jerry Bennett. Caleb Driscoll had the scantest of possessions – britches and shirts, his work gloves, a couple of blankets, and a Bible his grandmother had given him. Caleb kept those in Zeke's wagon because he drove Zeke's team. The Tucker boys, Johnny and Billy, brought wives along with them, and it seemed right that the women should call the wagon their own.

By the time the Tuckers' wagon was down, the trail along the top of the ridge had turned to so much mud that they gave up using the team of oxen and instead added three more men to each of the rope teams. No hand would be spared blisters this day.

The Grants, the Gordons, the Barneses. Three more wagons made it down into the canyon. They got another of Elias's wagons down into the canyon. His daughter Maggie and her new husband Jason Winter were in a wagon Elias had provided to them. It had become the family's wagon, though, after Elias had lost his own to the Snake River. They'd salvaged the strongbox with the money, but not much else was saved. Foodstuffs were all gone. A couple of blankets, some clothes. But Elias wanted to get Jason Winter's wagon into the canyon. His own family would gather at that wagon and camp there at it. That would put Elias down in the canyon to deal with any problem that might arise. Zeke would still be up top, camped with those wagons that would have to wait for the next day to go down the slope.

They got Luke Suttles's wagon down into the canyon. But by then, the temperature was beginning to drop as the sun disappeared behind the opposite slope, and folks were getting exhausted.

Elias called an end to the day's work.

The families whose wagons had gone down now followed the switch-back trail the animals had taken earlier in the day. Mothers held tight to their small children and tisked their tongues at the vast quantities of mud caked to everything.

Elias found Zeke resting on a rock among the pines.

"You keep an eye on things up top tonight?"

Zeke nodded his head.

"You think we can get all the rest of the wagons down tomorrow?" Zeke asked.

Elias looked at the long line of wagons still waiting to go.

"I hope so," he said. "I'll see you in the morning."

He took his wife Maddie by the arm and walked her down the switch-back trail.

"Everything is covered in mud," Maddie said. "Before it was dust. And then it was sand. And now it's mud."

Elias chuckled.

"We'll be out of these mountains soon," he promised.

"Then it will be one more thing," Maddie said, sounding exasperated. She sniffed a little, and Elias thought it was just the cold. But then he glanced at her and saw her eyes were wet.

"Oh, Maddie. Don't cry," he whispered. "We've got to keep people's spirits up."

A hand flew to her face, her mitten swiping across first one eye and then the other. She sniffed again, but as she lowered her hand, Elias could see a stiff resolve.

"I'm not crying," she said. "I'm just tired. I'm tired of walking. I'm tired of being hot, and now I'm tired of being cold. I'm tired of cooking on a campfire, and I'm tired of washing laundry in a creek."

She nodded forward to Sophie Bloom who would be giving birth in another three months. She navigated the switchback trail with a swollen belly, holding a child's hand in each of her own, with Cody Page holding her other child's hand and one hand on her upper arm to keep her steady.

"Look at that poor woman," Maddie said. "At least our children are grown. The girls are helping, the boys think they're on some grand adventure and are loving every moment of it. At least I don't have her troubles. Widowed, pregnant – doing all of this and doing everything for her children with no help."

"Cody's helping her," Elias said, feeling defensive. He thought he'd done right by having Cody take charge of Mrs. Bloom's wagon.

"It's not the same as having a husband. I look at Mrs. Bloom and her misfortunes, and I know I shouldn't complain."

"There's plenty to complain about," Elias said. "But we knew it would be hard."

Maddie scoffed.

"It's one thing to sit in your home in Paducah and say, 'this will be hard' with a warm stove and plenty of firewood and a cellar stocked with food and family and neighbors close by and your shoes not worn paper thin. It's something else to be here and know what hard is."

The loss of their wagon also meant the loss of provisions. Flour, beans, rice, sugar, coffee, potatoes, onions – so much given over to the Snake River. On purpose, Elias and his wife had oversupplied. Adding Zeke's wagon, Elias's family and hired men accounted at the start of the journey for five wagons and twenty souls among this wagon train. At camp, Maddie often fed some or all of those people, though Zeke and Marie usually kept their own, and Jason and Maggie, the newlyweds, most often did, too. But the hired hands, even the two Tucker brothers who were both married and with their wives on this journey, often took their meals with Elias and his family. Fortunately, they'd spread their supplies out over four of those five wagons. Still, the bulk of what they had left to get them to Oregon City had gone under when they lost the wagon.

Their oldest daughter, Maggie, pitched in. Both the Tucker women did, as well. Marie, Zeke's wife, started feeding some of the hired men from her own supplies. Others in the wagon train also helped. Elias's hired men were doing most of the work in tending to the livestock, along with some of the men in the wagon train who were packing west, and now families here and there would share a meal with Jerry Bennett or one of the Page brothers. Cody Page, who was driving Sophie Bloom's team, ate mostly from Mrs. Bloom's supplies, now.

"How is the food holding out?" Elias asked his wife while he made the campfire and she prepared to cook supper.

"We're almost out of flour," Maddie said. "We're completely out of sugar and coffee. We have rice enough, and beans, but the only things that seem plentiful enough to last until we get to The Dalles are the butter and the jerky."

Elias nodded his head.

"I'm glad we took the time to butcher those two steers down in the valley and smoke the meat."

A few among the emigrants had been against it. They lost three days of travel, but every family in the wagon train now had sufficient meat.

While Elias worked on the campfire and Madeline cut potatoes, Gloria Barnes came to their wagon with an empty jar.

"I hate to bother, Mrs. Townes," she said. "But do you have any preserves? We've run out, and without realizing it, I'd promised the girls biscuits and preserves."

31

Maddie glanced at Elias who gave her a small nod. The Barnes family had lost a daughter to violence committed by a man Elias had hired on as a guide. Elias bore a sense of guilt over that. While the Barnes family received a general sympathy from everyone among the emigrant train, Elias would have given them anything he had to make amends.

"Let me look," Maddie said, climbing into the wagon where they could hear her rummaging. She appeared a moment later with two jars.

"We have two jars. The strawberry preserves are open, but it's almost a full jar," Maddie said. "The peach preserves haven't been opened. Which would you prefer?"

"If I could just take some of the strawberry, the girls would be delighted by that."

"Take the jar," Maddie said.

"Oh, I couldn't take so much. But I'd happily pay you for – half? – of what you have there?"

"Please, take the jar," Maddie said. "No need to pay me for it. I'm just glad I have enough to help."

"Do you need anything?" Gloria Barnes asked. "We still have quite a bit of flour and rice."

"We're okay for the moment," Maddie said. "But don't be surprised if I ask for a little flour before we reach Oregon City."

"I thought you said we were low on flour," Elias said. "She offered some."

Maddie nodded her head.

"I'll know who to ask when we need some," Maddie said. "For now, I'll be generous with what we have so that I don't feel bad when the time comes that I need to rely on others' generosity."

"Huh. When the time comes, we may be lucky to find any generosity."

4

THE ACCIDENT CAME MIDMORNING.

The emigrants began early lowering the wagons, and they'd made good progress. After six wagons were down, Elias and some of those who'd started the day on the canyon floor climbed the switchback trail to put their backs into the hard work of lowering wagons.

They had Jeb Smith's wagon tied into the pulleys and had just gotten it over the precipice when one of the ropes around the wagon snapped. The sudden jerk of the full weight of the wagon toppled the men holding the other rope, and they scattered clear as the rope whipped through the pulley. The wheels of the wagon had been bound and locked in place, but that made no difference to gravity. With the mud greasing the slope, the wagon's wheels acted like skids, and the thing slid, picking up speed until it skidded off the path, struck a rock and flipped.

With an almighty crash, the wagon toppled over itself, breaking apart as it rolled down the steep incline, scattering Jeb Smith's possessions and provisions all down the hillside.

The men at the top of the canyon rim who'd scattered clear of the rope now collected themselves, knocked the mud from their clothes if they'd gone to ground. Some of them made their way to the precipice to take a look down below at the shattered wagon.

Jeb Smith's elderly father, Hezekiah, did not wait for anyone to decide what to do next. He started down the switchback path almost the moment the wagon reached the canyon floor, collecting what could be salvaged. Clothes, bags of rice and beans, jerky wrapped in cheesecloth, all sorts of provisions and tools.

"We can help you with that," Elias called to him. The elderly man waved his hand without looking back – a dismissive gesture.

Jeb Smith, though, was in no mood to dismiss anything. He'd stood with the others at the edge of the slope, looking down at his smashed wagon, but now he turned on Elias.

"You lost your own wagon, and now you're trying to destroy everyone else's!" Jeb Smith shouted the accusation at Elias.

"Now hold on," Elias said.

But Smith was running hot, jabbing his finger at Elias, shouting expletives and accusations.

Stephen Barnes was the first to come to Elias's defense.

"Mr. Smith, I assure you, this wasn't Elias's fault. I was on the rope beside him. There's no way that he could do anything to cause this or prevent it. A rope broke. That's all."

"His brother is on one rope and he's on the other!" Smith said, as if that was some damning evidence.

"Who secured your wagon, Mr. Smith?" Barnes demanded. "Who should have seen that the rope was weak and wouldn't hold?"

The two men were almost nose-to-nose, shouting at each other. Elias stepped in between them, gently pushing Barnes back. Zeke came near, standing just behind Smith and ready to grab the man if he should become violent.

"It's an unfortunate accident, Mr. Smith, and nothing more than that," Elias said. "We should collect your supplies and then go inspect the wagon to see if it can be repaired."

"Repaired? Is that a joke? You've seen it down there. It can't be repaired."

Several men were gathered near now. Women had taken their small children farther back at Smith's liberal use of language. Captain Walker and Walter Brown had both put a hand on Smith, gently trying to back him away.

"It's just one bit of trouble after another with you. Ain't it, Townes?" Smith persisted.

"Mr. Smith, it was an unfortunate accident, and none of us have been spared unfortunate accidents. Come on, and I'll help you salvage what can be salvaged from your provisions."

"And do what with them?" Smith demanded. "Am I to carry all my things on my back now?"

Elias turned his back on the man, muttering as he did, "We'll make arrangements."

But turning his back proved too much to take for Jeb Smith. The man launched himself at Elias, throwing a forearm into the back of Elias's head. Both men went over in a heap into the mud.

The Townes brothers were big men, tall and naturally strong with broad shoulders. All the men in their family were. And the fact that they earned their keep swinging axes, working band saws, and toting tree trunks and boards added significantly to the strength nature had given them.

So when Jeb Smith went for Elias with his back turned, Zeke rushed forward, grabbed Smith by the top of his britches and the collar of his shirt, and he lifted the man off his brother before more damage could be done.

He slung Smith away, sending him headlong into the thickest part of the mud.

Captain Walker and Stephen Barnes quickly grabbed Elias by the shoulders and helped him to his feet, but they also pulled him back, off the trail and into the trees, and held him so that he wouldn't return violence with violence. But Elias had no intention of it.

The fight was out of Smith, too.

The man picked himself up from the mud, wiping it from his face and hands and trying to knock it off his clothes.

"I understand you're upset," Elias said to him. "I'll let that pass, Mr. Smith. But if you fail to control your temper again – whether with me or anyone else in this wagon train – you'll find yourself banished."

"And good riddance to you," Captain Walker said.

5

"I DON'T LIKE THE look of those clouds," Elias said, covering his eyes against the glare of the sky.

"Nor do I," Zeke agreed.

Up ahead, the sound of ax heads striking timber rang out. Every man who could swing and ax was throwing his back into the work. The boys too young to fell the big spruce and pines cut saplings. Henry Blair had gone off on his own, looking for the missing trail.

"We must have lost it when we came up out of the canyon," Zeke said.

They'd followed a draw up to a high ridge that took them out of the tree line, across the peak of a bald mountaintop. The snow there had hidden the trail, but they managed to follow the natural contour of the land, believing that was the way the trail would take them. Now, though, they'd dipped back down into the trees and soon found themselves on a path too narrow for the wagons. Every man took up an ax and went ahead of the wagon trail, dropping trees that impeded the trail.

"If those are snow clouds, Elias, we'll have to abandon the wagons."

They'd come down a steep incline that required ropes and chains again, and at the bottom were forced to ford a shallow creek. It was mercifully narrow, but it moved fast and more than one wagon was nearly lost to the current. It had been a day's work getting down the incline and across the creek. But there the trail had been wide and on roughly level ground down in another canyon, giving them hope that they were still on the right path. But when it narrowed and there was no way for wagons to get through, they knew for sure they'd wandered off the trail.

"Maybe Henry will come back with good news," Elias said. "Maybe we're close to being out of the mountains."

They canyon took them down between high hills, mountain spurs. The creek cut north and west at first, but now they were winding to the east, curling around a mountain spur, and moving at a snail's pace as the clap and thud of axes working in front of them continued to drop trees. The hills above were mostly bare of trees, other than a stand here and there or a single tree. But the inclines were steep and they could find no obvious ridge that would allow them to travel from one hill to the next without have to drop down into narrow canyons.

They'd talked about turning around and going back, trying to find the trail now that the snow had melted some. But no option seemed better than another, and at least until they heard from Henry Blair, Elias was determined to press on. He reasoned that this creek had to find its way out into the valley west of the Blue Mountains.

"You've got other problems, too," Zeke said.

"Do I?"

"Hezekiah Smith is making noise that his son Jeb should be captain of the wagon train. Captain Walker told me that Hezekiah said as much to him last night."

Elias frowned.

"If Jeb Smith wants to lead the wagon train, he's welcome to it. I wouldn't stand in the way of anyone who wants to follow him."

"That's what I told Captain Walker," Zeke said. "These folks wouldn't make it ten miles without you leading them. I also told Captain Walker that if they get themselves in a bind, they'd better not expect us to come back for them."

Elias nodded his head.

"Is anyone thinking about following Jeb Smith?"

"Captain Walker is not," Zeke said. "I couldn't tell you if anyone else is thinking about it."

"If we didn't have our entire livelihood in that wagon, I'd say right now you and me and everyone with us should abandon our wagons and pack out of here. We could be in Oregon City in under two weeks."

"Doesn't do us any good to get to Oregon City if we can't cut trees for a living," Zeke said.

Somewhere up ahead on the trail someone called out a warning. Then they heard the familiar crack and splinter as a tree ripped free of whatever thin bit of wood still held it in place. They heard the tree fall through its neighbors, snapping limbs as it went down, and the crash as it hit the ground.

"That was a big one," Elias said.

"Too bad we can't cut boards as we go," Zeke chuckled. "We could show up in Oregon City with a load of fresh boards and start turning a profit on day one."

Elias grabbed the handle of his ax, leaning now against the trunk of a tree they wouldn't have to drop.

"I'd better get back at it," he said.

"Me, too," Zeke said, grabbing his own ax. "Anything you want me to do about Jeb Smith?"

"Do?" Elias said. "Like what?"

"I could talk to the other folks, campaign on your behalf. I could pull him aside and tell him to drop it – we're almost there and he doesn't need to start trouble now."

"No," Elias said. "Let him be. If he wants to campaign against me, that's fine. If some of the others folks decide to follow him and strike off on their own, that's fine. Let them do what they want to do."

MARCUS WEISS USED HIS ax to knock down some of the saplings growing in the middle of the trail or along the edges. Felling trees wasn't along his line. He reasoned there were others more capable of that work, and so he would leave them to it.

"It's a helluva thing, having to cut down a forest and make our own trail," Jeb Smith said, walking up to Weiss and wiping the sweat from his own brow. Smith had been farther up the trail, and the wet stains on his shirt suggested he'd been chopping down something more significant than saplings.

"It's that damned Elias Townes," Weiss said. "He lost the trail. We'll be lucky to get out of these mountains before another snow."

Smith nodded his head, looking up through the canopy.

"If those are snow clouds, we'll be cutting down trees and fighting a blizzard all at the same time. We should have replaced Townes as the wagon train's captain back on the Snake River when he hired guides who tried to murder us."

"Every step he's taken has been wrong-footed," Weiss said. "The trouble is, there's no will among these people to do anything for themselves. They'll all blindly follow Townes to their own destruction."

Wiser McKinney was standing within earshot of the two men as they spoke. Like Weiss, Wiser wasn't handy at chopping down large trees. But he'd knocked down a couple of smaller pines and had helped cut the trunk of a bigger tree into manageable pieces and then helped drag those pieces off the trail.

"You two should get to work," Wiser said. "I've heard what you've said about Elias Townes, and I can say with certainty that you're in a very small minority with your complaints. Those men Elias hired at Bridger's Fort? He had no way of knowing what they intended. When we lost the trail, I didn't hear either of you pointing out that we were going the wrong way. Anyone could have lost that trail in the snow, and every one of us is as guilty as Elias. Instead of bellyaching, you should pitch in and help us clear this trail so the wagons can get through. Anything else you do is a waste of time."

"Come on, Wiser," Smith said. "Every other wagon train making this journey has moved along the trail without half the problems. If you're honest with yourself, you'll acknowledge that Elias Townes is incapable, and he's putting the rest of us at risk with his incompetence."

"You're just angry because of what happened to your wagon," Wiser said. "But don't forget, Elias lost a wagon, too."

"Does that make it okay that I lost my property?" Smith asked. "Not in my mind."

"My point is that accidents happen," Wiser said.

"I doubt you'd be so charitable if the accident deprived you of your property," Smith said.

"I'm sure I wouldn't be at all pleased," Wiser said. "But I also wouldn't blame someone else who had no fault in it. Mr. Townes is doing what he can to get us all safely to Oregon City, and I trust him to do it."

"All of us safely?" Jeb Smith said, his voice dripping with incredulity. "What about Sophie Bloom, now missing a husband buried along the trail? John Long, also dead. And we have no idea what became of Reverend Marsh and his wife."

"Don't forget the Barnes girl, buried along the Snake River," Marcus Weiss added. "Or my hired man, Butch – murdered by Zeke Townes."

"And I'd hardly consider myself safely arrived at Oregon City when I consider the loss of my personal belongings," Jeb Smith added.

"Every wagon train that's ever crossed the plains has encountered its share of difficulty and loss. Our experiences are nothing outside of the norm. In fact, we've probably made it thus far with fewer troubles than many."

The argument among the three men began to draw attention from others nearby.

Grant, and his two older sons, left their work to come and listen. John Gordon, whose wife made herself a constant irritant in the wagon train by spreading rumors, quickly took up Jeb Smith's side.

"You're arguing about what's done in the past and cannot be changed," John Gordon said. "But my concern is right here and now – we're lost!"

Stephen Barnes, though he had lost a daughter to violence, remained a staunch defender of Elias Townes, and Hezekiah Smith, Jeb's father, now engaged in a separate argument with Barnes.

"If anyone should question the wisdom of Mr. Townes, it should be you, Barnes," Hezekiah Smith said. "He hired the men who killed your daughter."

"He hired the only men available at Bridger's Fort. He knew we needed guides to see us through the last part of the journey."

Old as he was, Hezekiah didn't mind jabbing Stephen Barnes in the chest with a bent finger.

"If somebody doesn't take charge of this wagon train, we'll all die in these mountains, Barnes," Hezekiah told him.

It went on like this for several minutes when Solomon McKinney at last raised his voice and put an abrupt end to the discussion.

"Whether Elias Townes is the most competent man to lead us to Oregon City or not, I know one thing for certain," Solomon said. "He's not here defending himself because he's busy clearing a trail so that we can get out of these mountains. While you men are standing around debating his fitness, he's actually doing something."

"Well, that's an end to that," Wiser said, with a nod to his brother. "Let's get back to work."

But even as the men spoke, the snow began to fall again.

6

A COLD WIND BLEW, and Henry shivered at its ominous import.

Henry Blair came west four years ago. He'd still been a teenager then. Sixteen.

He'd come along with a group of trappers. There wasn't money in beaver much anymore, but he'd been desperate, and an outfit out of St. Louis had backed the men. A sure payday if they brought back enough pelts. The men he traveled and trapped with were experienced. Most of them had made one or two trips west. A couple of them had made more than that. They were old Hudson Bay Company men.

They'd trapped in the Wind River Mountains and wintered at Bridger's Fort. During a winter excursion, they'd been trapped in a blizzard in the mountains south of Bridger's. Henry shivered to think about it now. Two of the men he'd been with died of exposure, and as they fought their way out of the blizzard to return to the fort, they'd come across a little settlement of Indians, most of them on the verge of starvation. There had been a fight as the starving Indians attempted to take what provisions the trappers had. But it wasn't much of a fight. One of the men with Henry was clubbed to death, but when the trappers unleashed a volley with their rifles, the Indians scattered.

Henry decided then he'd never come west again if he ever made it home. And he intended to keep that promise. But times were hard back in St. Joseph. He'd worked what odd jobs he could find for wages insufficient to keep him fed and housed, often skipping meals to rent a room. And this opportunity came along. He'd been honest and up front with the Townes brothers when they came to him in St. Jo. I only been as far as Bridger's Fort, he told them. I can't guide you beyond there.

They'd hired him on anyway. They'd said they'd been told the trail was well marked. They needed a man who'd been west, dealt with the Plains Indians, understood the lay of the land.

Henry told them he could do those things.

The price they offered to serve as a guide, it was more money than Henry could hope to make in a year. Of course he'd signed on. There was also a hint of opportunity at the end of the trail. The Townes brothers intended to start a logging operation. They were building a sawmill and would have to hire on men.

But he'd never guessed he'd find himself alone on a trail through the mountains.

Now, he was haunted by the memory of those starving Indians. Their faces contorted with hunger. They'd have done anything to get at the little provisions Henry had. They'd have killed him to butcher his horse and mule. The memory filled his chest, twisted his gut. How would he handle an encounter now?

He'd not been among the men quick to load and fire a rifle on that day four years ago. The others, those hard men he'd ridden with, they reacted. Henry did not. Scared for his life, his hands shaking, he could do nothing more that day than grab his rifle like a club.

He remembered that fear so clearly now, like ice around his heart and in his veins. He remembered it so clearly because it was the same fear that returned to him at this moment.

Alone. Deep in a mountain forest. Lost. Maybe no white man had ever even been here before. But he was on a trail, all the same. Someone had been here before. Someone had used this trail many times.

Somewhere nearby in the forest over Henry Blair's left shoulder, some massive thing crashed through the undergrowth.

Henry jumped in the saddle, startled by the noise. His hand shot for the knife on his belt, and he wrapped his fingers tight around the grip, holding his breath. The horse heard it too and dropped his head spinning as he did. The great beast was too big for such a sudden maneuver, and he stumbled making it. Henry pulled on the reins, bringing the horse's head back up.

An elk burst forth from the darkness behind the evergreens, his massive rack seemingly pushing the trees right out of his way. He bounded across the trail, hardly sparing a look for the young man fighting to right his panicked horse. Then the elk dashed off into the trees on the opposite side of the trail.

Henry had the horse under control now. He let go of his knife and put a hand on the horse's neck.

"It's all right, now," Henry said, laughing at himself and the way his stomach had lurched.

The quiet of the forest, the loneliness being out here on his own, it all played on Henry's imagination. Every bush was a grizzly bear. Every tree trunk, a hostile Indian looking for a scalp. So when he heard the elk, Henry was certain some danger had come for him.

He was still laughing when he realized that a half dozen men or more had stepped out of the woods and surrounded him. They were armed with bows and hatchets. Each of them had long black hair, braided. They wore animal skins fashioned into britches and shirts, the skins were dark, like their exposed faces and arms.

The men looked at Henry for a long moment, and Henry looked back at them. The thought running through his mind was to flee, to wheel his horse and charge past the men. He would absorb whatever blows they sent at him, but so long as he could maintain the saddle and get through, he'd be fine.

And then one of the men said, "You lost."

Henry blinked his eyes to hear English spoken to him from this strange face in a place that seemed so far away from anywhere that people spoke English.

"I am lost," Henry admitted.

"I am Tu Ah Tway. I am a chief among the Liksiyu People."

The man spoke with an accent. The words clearly came to him unnaturally, but he was clear enough to understand.

"I'm trying to reach the mission at The Dalles," Henry said. "I'm traveling the emigrant trail with a wagon train."

"No," Tu Ah Tway said. "You have come far from the trail."

"We got turned around in the snow," Henry said. "We lost the trail. My people are behind me."

"This is an old hunting trail," Tu Ah Tway said. "You are in my people's hunting grounds. My people have used this trail, many years. Long before my time."

"We're not intending to trespass," Henry said, still concerned for his scalp, though feeling a mite better that the man spoke to him in his own language.

Now the group of men began talking to each other in their own tongue, and one of them reached up and took the bridle of Henry's horse. Henry watched the leisurely way the man held the horse there. He never looked at Henry when he took hold of the bridle and continued now to ignore him. Henry could only follow the tone of the discussion, but he sensed at least a couple of the men were unhappy with him being on the trail. The others didn't seem to be defending him. He'd heard Indians talk in their own language plenty of times – at Bridger's Fort when whites and Indians often congregated together, on the trail when they came to the wagons to barter or sell. He always thought their clipped words sounded harsh and angry, but they'd never put him so afeared as they did now.

"Listen, I'm just trying to find a way out of these mountains," Henry said to Tu Ah Tway, guessing he was the only one among them who spoke English. "My folks back at the wagon train, they got turned around in the snow. We've come the wrong way. We're looking for a way down into the valley."

"You go to the mission?" Tu Ah Tway said. "Baxter?"

There was a name Henry recognized. He'd heard the Baxter's talked about before. There'd been a Methodist preacher in the wagon train before the man took ill and turned back to winter at one of the forts. Rev. Marsh and his wife intended to preach to the Natives, and Marsh had spoken of the Baxter mission. Henry had heard the Baxters talked about at Fort Bridger, too, when he'd come that way as a trapper. Narcissa Baxter was famous for being among the first women to make the overland journey more than a decade ago. Henry put Tu Ah Tway's English together with his knowledge of the mission, and gambled that maybe the Indian was friendly and could help them.

"That's right," Henry said. "The mission. We need to get to the mission."

"This creek," Tu Ah Tway said, motioning in the direction of the creek flowing through the canyon. "It meets river. Follow river into valley. North to mission."

Henry touched his hat and nodded his head, but the man holding his horse's bridle did not turn it loose. Now there was more discussion among the Indians. They seemed to be arguing about something. Finally, Tu Ah Tway turned back to Henry.

"Take us to wagons. We will take you to the mission."

AFTER TU AH TWAY and the others with him gathered their horses from where they'd left them when they started after the elk, Henry Blair turned back toward the wagon train.

That anxious feeling didn't leave him, though he felt certain if they intended to kill him, they would have done it by now. If they were thinking they could steal from the wagon train, they'd have another idea of it when they got back to the others and the Indians saw the numbers of settlers. Still, Henry didn't like being outnumbered by men he didn't know and couldn't trust.

They didn't talk much, especially at the beginning of the ride, and when there was any communication, it came from their chief. The others seemed to understand well enough, and so Henry guessed they had at least some English. His guess was confirmed along the ride back to the wagon train when Tu Ah Tway introduced them as Joshua, James, John, Paul, and Peter.

"Those are all English names," Henry said.

49

"Those are the English names given to them by Baxter," Tu Ah Tway said. "He calls me Adam."

The native men were jovial as they rode along the trail, making jokes in their own tongue and laughing. But sometimes they shared the jokes with Henry in their broken English. Henry didn't think any of the jokes were particularly humorous, but they did help in relieving his tension, putting him at ease with his new acquaintances. Men who joked and rode along with him probably did not intend to offer any aggression.

Tu Ah Tway, the one who seemed to be in charge and did all the talking, he asked Henry many questions about Jesus and salvation – questions Henry didn't feel at all able to answer. But the Indian was very curious about how one man's suffering and death could purify every other man's soul. Tu Ah Tway said the women at the mission sometimes wept when they spoke of Jesus. What troubled Tu Ah Tway most was that so far as he could understand, Jesus had not been a great warrior and had won no battles against his enemies.

"I think his victory was in his sacrifice," Henry offered.

"That is what Baxter says," Tu Ah Tway said. "But there is no great victory in falling to your enemies."

Henry sighed.

"It's not a thing I know a lot about," he admitted. "But the Bible tells us that Jesus rose from the dead. If your enemies kill you, and then you come back to life, that's a victory."

Tu Ah Tway meditated on this for a moment.

"When he came back to life, did he kill the men who put him on the cross?"

"No," Henry said. "He forgave them."

"And do you follow this man, Jesus?" Tu Ah Tway asked.

"I don't think about it much. But I reckon I try to."

"A great spirit, all powerful, that dies as a man," Tu Ah Tway said. "Your David. Now that was a man to follow. Mighty warrior. Many women."

Henry nodded along. He knew something about David being a warrior, but he didn't know so much about David and women.

"If your God should be a man, he should have been David," Tu Ah Tway said, narrowing his eyes and watching for Henry's reaction.

"Maybe," Henry said. "But ain't many of us know what it's like to be a king like David was. I reckon God had to be Jesus because most of us understand him better. Jesus was just like us. Folks shunned him, he was poor and meek. He got angry sometimes and felt misunderstood, even by his friends. When I think of Jesus, I think that's somebody I could know. But David was a king. I couldn't know him any more than I could know the president of the United States."

Tu Ah Tway dropped the subject at that, leaving Henry with the impression that he wasn't entirely satisfied at the answers Henry had to give.

The stories from the Bible were things Henry grew up with, taught to him mostly by his mother before she died when he was still young. He wondered what these Indians must have thought when the missionaries came to them telling them to worship a man who gave up his life and preached forgiveness to their enemies. Tu Aw Tway had been among the missionaries long enough that his English was pretty good, but he still seemed confounded by the religion that compelled the missionaries to teach him English in the first place.

At last, Henry asked the question that had been burning inside him.

"How far are we from the mission?"

"Two, maybe three days on horseback," Tu Ah Tway said. "With your wagons, five or six days."

Under a week! It seemed unreal that they could be so near to salvation. Henry's first thought was how relieved he would feel if Elias would agree to abandon the wagons and reach the mission in two or three days. But he knew Elias would never give up the wagons, not now. But five or six days? The disappearing rations need not be a worry anymore. The fast approaching winter months, neither. All the troubles that had plagued them these last few weeks now seemed to evaporate.

By now it was beginning to snow, but Henry didn't worry about that. Even if it snowed five or six inches, they'd still be able to get the wagons out through this trail. And they had guides now who knew the way to the mission. Once they got to the mission, they would be able to get to Oregon City, Henry was confident of that. There were settlements here, he knew. The Baxter mission was one, but there was also a larger settlement at The Dalles, and Henry didn't doubt there were more that he knew nothing about. Tu Ah Tway and his friends meant the Townes Party was saved, even if they didn't arrive in Oregon City until spring.

As they rode, the clouds began rolling in thicker and darker. The snow began to fall. The light of day started to fade, especially down in the canyon.

Henry didn't know how far back the pioneers might be. He'd left them the previous day and camped alone on the trail. When he first encountered Tu Ah Tway, he thought that maybe he could reach the wagons before dark, but as the day grew short, a new worry came on Henry. He still didn't entirely trust these Indians escorting him, and he did not want to be forced into camping alone with them. With each step the horses took, Henry said a silent prayer that they would reach the Townes Party before dark.

7

DOWN IN THE CANYON, the snow wasn't so bad. But through the canopy of the trees, on the bare hillsides above them, the settlers could see it accumulating thick. It had come down heavy through the night and left about two inches on the trail.

"It's still snowing, though," Jeb Smith said when Wiser McKinney pointed out that they wouldn't have any difficulty moving the wagons through two inches of snow. "It could be five inches by nightfall, and ten tomorrow morning. And what if it gets worse?"

"What if it stops?" Wiser said. "Mr. Smith, you've got to stop borrowing trouble. All we can do is keep moving."

Elias figured they'd cleared the trail wide enough to move the wagons at least two miles the previous day, and at that point the forest seemed to recede from the trail at least enough to keep the wagons going for some distance. He sent his son-in-law Jason Winter and Zeke ahead on horseback to take a look at the trail, to see how far they could make it with the wagons before they would have to take out trees again. Zeke rode with an ax so that if he encountered saplings or smaller trees interrupting the path, he could take them down ahead of the wagons.

The animals were moving now, the oxen pulling the wagons, the livestock back behind them. They'd been going for an hour already. It was slow.

The oxen seemed none too interested in pulling the wagons. Whether it was the cold or a lack of strength – forage in the mountains had been poor and the animals showed their exhaustion. The pioneers, too, were slow moving. The children were cold and complaining, their mothers and fathers lacked the energy to even argue with them. Every step seemed to take all any of them had, and then they had to conjure the strength for the next step.

Only Zeke's dogs possessed any energy to run ahead of the wagon train or chase through the woods. The dogs enjoyed the snow and didn't mind the cold.

Elias was walking now, his horse Tuckee tied behind the wagon his son Gabriel drove. When they came on tight spots, where the trees or stumps made the trail almost impassable, Elias and his son Christian would help guide the wagons to make sure the wheels didn't run up on a stump. A broken wheel – or worse, a broken axle – would delay them hours. This far into the journey, there were few spare wheels remaining in the wagon train, and those who had one were unlikely to part with it if someone else lost a wheel. When they'd started this journey, everyone was happy to share what they had if their neighbor was in need. Now, everyone was a bit more guarded about what was theirs.

"We've got one stuck!" came a shout from somewhere near the back.

Elias and Christian had been guiding wagons through a narrow space, and Elias looked at Christian now.

"You watch these wagons closely. Make sure they take this straight on," he told his son. "I'm going to go back and see what I can do to help."

He walked along the line of wagons. Most folks were turned around looking, but no one was going back to lend a hand. At last he came to the stuck wagon and found Marcus Weiss's wagon up to its axle in mud where it had run off the path.

Caleb Driscoll, who drove Zeke's wagon and was last in the line of wagons, had already taken an ax and begun skinning small branches off a tree they'd cut down the previous day. He'd placed a couple of the branches in the mud at the front of the stuck wheel, hoping to give the wheel something more solid from which to roll out of the mud.

Jerry Bennett, who rode with the cow column, now came up on his horse. He grabbed a second ax and started chopping at the trunk of a small pine, about four or five inches in diameter. Again, this was a tree they'd cut down the previous day to make room for the wagons. He was cutting off a length about twenty feet long to use as a lever. Four or five strong men working one end of that pine would probably be able to lift the back corner of the wagon enough that with Caleb's branches the oxen would be able to pull the wagon clear.

Marcus Weiss, meanwhile, stood at the front of his wagon, whip in hand, watching Caleb work.

"If it's not one thing, it's another. Eh, Mr. Weiss," Elias said, trying to be genial.

The truth was, Elias despised Marcus Weiss. The troubles with the man started early, all the way back along the Platte River, when the wagon train had passed an Indian burial site. The Natives there didn't bury their dead, but instead erected a scaffolding and left their dead to be scattered by the birds and the wind. Weiss had climbed the scaffolding and pulled away a souvenir, some piece of ornamental jewelry that had been left on the dead man.

Several people among the wagon train had objected, including Elias who insisted that Weiss return the stolen trinket. But Weiss refused. Elias worried for days that some Indian might have seen Weiss and his actions would be enough to get them attacked. No attack ever came, but the incident set the tone. Several times, almost nightly, Weiss fought with his wife. He'd laid hands on her a number of times. It was Zeke who finally said something to the man, offering to return whatever violence Weiss imposed on his wife. That stopped it, though the man's attitude toward her was often cruel, he'd not hit her since Zeke threatened him.

And then there'd been the incident between Fort Laramie and the South Pass. An altercation between Zeke and Weiss's driver that led to violence. Elias hadn't witnessed it, but those who did – including Zeke – said his actions had been in self-defense. Weiss called it murder and demanded that Zeke be hanged. There'd been no hanging, but for almost five hundred miles, Zeke traveled alone after being banished from the wagon train.

Still, Elias tried to be genial. He'd thought Weiss would leave the wagon train at Bridger's Fort, but he'd been unable to join any other wagon train, mostly because Weiss himself bickered about the cost to buy a spot. Elias figured if he was stuck with Weiss, he'd at least try to keep it civil.

"If it's not one thing, it's another because we're being led by incompetence," Weiss said.

Elias frowned at him.

"If you say so, Mr. Weiss. Either way, I'll get you out of this mud hole as quick as I can."

It didn't take long, either. A couple of the other men put their weight into the lever, along with Elias and Jerry Bennett. Caleb Driscoll and another man gave the wagon a push. Weiss got his oxen heaving against the weight. The wheel caught the branches Caleb had put down, and the wagon got rolling again.

That's when the shout came from up above that Zeke and Jason Winter were coming back. Elias gave Weiss's wagon a lingering look to make certain it wasn't headed off the path again, and then he hurried forward, wondering if his brother had more bad news. But as he neared the front, he heard someone say that Henry Blair was with Zeke, along with half a dozen Indians.

"I DIDN'T WANT TO camp with them," Henry Blair confessed to Zeke. "Honestly, I didn't close my eyes all night."

"I expect it was easy enough to stay awake," Zeke said. "It was a cold night last night, and you didn't have a tent."

"They cut pine branches and made little shelters for everyone. I stayed warm enough. But I was scared out of my mind that any minute they might decide to take my scalp."

Zeke nodded his head, paying less attention to Henry than to the conversation taking place several feet away.

"They seem friendly enough," Zeke said.

"Well, they didn't take my scalp," Henry conceded.

The conversation that most interested Zeke was the one between Tu Ah Tway and Elias. Some of the other men had gathered around to share their input – the McKinney brothers, John Gordon, Stephen Barnes, Captain Walker, and – notably – Jeb and Hezekiah Smith.

Zeke had stayed back a respectful distance, giving Elias the opportunity to have his parlay with the Indians. But the other men had gathered round uninvited.

"How bad do you expect this snowstorm to be?" Elias was asking.

Tu Ah Tway looked up at the dark clouds and the falling snow.

"Not so bad," Tu Ah Tway said. "Worse in the mountains. When we get down into the valley and near the mission there will be no snow."

"And this trail we're on?" Elias said. "Will it take us out of the mountains?"

Tu Ah Tway chuckled.

"You will have to chop down many more trees, but it will take you out of the mountains and down into the valley. You would be better off leaving the wagons."

Elias shook his head.

"We can't leave the wagons," he said. "We need the things we're carrying in the wagons."

Tu Ah Tway gave a skeptical look at the nearest wagons. He frowned at Elias and shook his head.

"The trail will take you to the Umatilla Valley, out of the mountains. When you're clear of the mountains, if you follow north, you will come to the mission. It is not so hard to find from here. But it could take many days to get out of the mountains. This trail is too – what's the word? Close."

Tu Ah Tway gestured with his hands to indicate a narrow path. Elias chewed his lip and glanced at the other settlers who stood nearby.

"Will you give us time to talk about it?" Elias said. "Let me and these other men talk it out?"

Tu Ah Tway nodded his head.

"Talk," he said.

Immediately all the settlers broke away into groups of three or four or more. Those who hadn't been near enough to hear the discussion with Tu Ah Tway now found someone who'd overheard the conversation. Elias went directly to Zeke.

"You've know I've been committed to leading this wagon train," Elias said. "But that wagon with our gear – that's our future, Zeke. I can't abandon our tools. It would be like abandoning the entire reason for making this journey. And it would be ridiculous to get one wagon to Oregon City and not the others."

For Elias, abandoning the wagons was an impossible option. He couldn't leave the wagon that carried the tools he needed to start his new business. He and Zeke had carefully budgeted everything. Wages for their hired men. The money it would take to build cabins, buy provisions and supplies – all the things they would require to get through a winter and set up the business. They'd planned every cost of the journey west, from buying the wagons and the supplies and the livestock to hiring a guide. All their planning and budgets included nothing for replacing the tools.

"What about this?" Elias said. "Send the women and children with Tu Ah Tway. Send enough men to keep them safe and pack out the supplies that they need. Leave some of the men back to keep the wagons moving. Anyone who wants to abandon their wagon can go on with Tu Ah Tway. Anyone who won't leave their wagon, they can stay back with me. We'll all meet up again at the mission."

"Split the wagon train," Zeke said, nodding his head. "Get the most vulnerable to safety. Still get the wagons out."

"It might mean a week or ten days of hard going for those back with the wagons, but the women and children will be safe in a couple of days."

Zeke nodded his head.

"All right. I'll stay back with the wagons."

Elias shook his head.

"No, brother. I want you to go with the women and children."

Zeke narrowed his eyes at Elias.

"I don't want to offend you Elias, but don't you think I'm better suited to stay back with the wagons?" Zeke said. "Look, Elias, you can work just as hard as me. Maybe harder. But we'll probably be cutting down trees every day, in addition to the labor just to keep the wagons moving down the path. We're talking about felling a lot of trees before we get out of these mountains. Let me do that work."

"I ain't so old that I can't chop down a tree, little brother," Elias said. "But it's not the work that worries me. If something goes wrong with those Indians, you're the one I trust most to be able to deal with it. You're handier with a gun than I am. Better in a fight. Don't laugh – it's not a pleasant thing for me to admit. But I'm thinking of sending my own wife and daughters ahead with these Indians. I need to know there's someone with them who can protect them."

Zeke chewed on that for a moment. Maybe there was truth in it. Zeke had fought an outfit of scalp hunters and a band of vengeful Indians back at South Pass. It wasn't like either of them had much experience in fighting – outside of a few drunken brawls outside a Paducah saloon that never amounted to much. But Zeke had proved his mettle, and both of them knew it.

"I'm going to propose the idea to the others. We'll need volunteers to go with you and the women and children. You'll also have any man who decides to abandon his wagon."

"Those will be the men least likely to be of much help to me," Zeke said.

"Probably," Elias agreed. "But we've got no reason to think these Indians will offer you trouble. They speak English, they're acquainted with the Baxter mission."

Elias began now gathering up the other men, bringing them into a consultation. There was immediate agreement among them that they should do whatever they could to spare the women and children from a tedious journey out of the mountains and into the Umatilla Valley. But no man said he was interested in leaving his wagon behind. Those who'd made it so far with their possessions – or most of their possessions – had no interest now in abandoning what they'd counted so dear for so long. They could see the end now, especially with the appearance of Tu Ah Tway and the other natives, who gave them hope that they would escape the mountains on this trail.

Jeb Smith and a couple of the men who were already packing their supplies and had no wagon agreed to go on ahead with Zeke and the women and children. But even Marcus Weiss refused to leave his wagon, and Elias suspected his would be the first voice volunteering to leave his possessions.

With some urging, Luke Suttle agreed to go. Luke was around Elias's age, and he was traveling with his nephew and his nephew's wife. His nephew could handle the wagon. Luke was a farmer back home and intended to farm in the Willamette Valley. Maybe not the best hand if it turned into a fight, but he was a strong man and old enough that he had some wisdom to lend.

Elias also persuaded Captain Walker, the veteran Indian fighter from the Seminole Wars. Elias said that he'd have his younger son, Christian, drive the captain's wagon.

And with some reluctance, Elias called both Henry Blair and Billy Tucker and told them to go on with Zeke. Billy's wife, Josie, she'd be going with the women and children, so Billy had a vested interest in keeping them safe. The Tucker brothers, Billy and Johnny, were two of Elias's best hands. He'd miss Billy when there were trees in the trail that needed to be dropped. But he also knew Billy was a solid man if there should be a fight. He sent Henry along because he could spare him. Henry helped with the cow column and was always the first one that Elias sent ahead to scout. But Elias could do the scouting himself.

They weren't much of a guard for the women. Zeke and Billy Tucker, Captain Walker and Luke Suttle. Those boys packing to Oregon were young and wiry and they'd probably be good men in a fight. Elias didn't know them well. They'd spent most of their time on the trail with the cow column.

But maybe the best part of it all would be getting Jeb Smith and his father away from the other men. Elias believed Jeb Smith was poison in the wagon train, and it would be a peaceful few days not having him whispering mutiny to the others.

"Maybe we'll be able to focus on pushing forward and getting into the valley," Elias told Zeke. "Now comes the hard part."

"What's the hard part?" Zeke asked.

"Convincing Maddie that she has to go on ahead and leave me with the wagons."

"No. I won't do it. I won't leave you," Madeline said.

"It's only a few days," Elias sighed. "It gets you out of these mountains and safely to the mission."

"We started this journey as a family. I intend to finish it that way," Maddie said.

"We will finish it that way," Elias promised her. "But supplies are running short. We have an opportunity now to get more than half the people in the wagon train to a safe place where they will be fed. And in a few days, we'll all be together again to finish out the journey."

"Why don't you come with us and let Zeke stay with the wagons? You didn't make a commitment to get the wagons to Oregon City. You made a commitment to get the people to Oregon City."

"That's why I'm sending Zeke. If something goes wrong with these Indians, I'd rather have Zeke there to deal with it. And we're only talking about a few days."

The word had spread by now through the entire wagon train. Similar conversations were taking place up and down the line of wagons. Some of the women greeted the plan with relief. The snow falling around them was concerning, and they all knew the lack of provisions that now affected every family. Others were like Madeline. Even if they saw the sense of it, they objected. Separation frightened them as much as the snow or the lack of supplies.

But they were also now dividing their stores. Leaving their husbands and sons with enough and gathering for themselves and their children who would be going. Already they were loading oxen and horses with supplies for the women and children.

"We need to get busy dividing up the provisions we have," Elias said to Maddie. "I understand you don't like it, but there's no choice in it. If you refuse to go, other women might also start to refuse. And then we're looking at a week or more of travel without sufficient supplies. As it is, those going on ahead need less and that leaves more for those staying with the wagons."

Maddie clenched her jaws and shook her head.

"All right, Elias. I'll go. But I do so under protest."

Tu Ah Tway and the other Indians patiently watched while the settlers made their arrangements. Without exception, the men packed their tents for their wives and children and decided they would make do sleeping in or under their wagons. They braced themselves for some cold, cramped nights. Zeke watched all this and wondered how many tents he would have to set up each night, how many packs he'd have to pack in the mornings. Most of the women were handy enough to do the work for themselves. If they hadn't been before the journey started, they'd learned on the way. But there were still a few who were accustomed to having their men do for them.

Elias solved another problem for himself. He'd started to worry that he wouldn't have men sufficient to keep the livestock, even with most of the horses in the party's remuda now getting saddled and some of the spare oxen toting packs with supplies.

He offered Tu Ah Tway half a dozen steers as payment for taking the women and children to the mission, and the Indian accepted. For Elias, it was better than paying with flour or sugar or corn meal – the stores of which were all dangerously low – or even gold or silver. And it alleviated at least some of the burden on the cow column.

Those men without wives – Jerry Bennett and the Page brothers and a few others – were already back at work clearing the trail. It was wider here, and they could walk some distance before finding a tree that had to be taken down to make the trail passable for the wagons. So even as the Indians mounted their horses and the women and children who had horses to ride also mounted, the did so with the music of the axes cutting through the forest.

The husbands and fathers stood to watch their families set out ahead of the wagons before getting to work to join them as quickly as possible.

8

THE SNOW FELL HEAVIER on the trail than it did under the canopy of trees.

As Elias rode Tuckee out in front of the wagons, the snow was almost pristine. Only four to six inches thick, but so much had fallen that it was hard now to find the tracks of those among the Townes party who'd gone out ahead of the wagons. Here and there he would see an indent in the snow and think that was probably a footprint two days ago but had now filled in.

It was snowing again now. When the trail wandered over beside the creek and there was enough break in the trees for Elias to see the mountains looming over him, he could tell that the snow was thicker up higher. Under the canopy of the trees, he could still catch glimpses of bare ground, though there wasn't much of that, now. They had a definite blanket of snow. They could get through it. The oxen could walk through it and the wagon wheels would roll through it. Fortunately, it was soft and powdery.

Behind them, the snow was slushy and muddy, and the trail was a mess.

The cold didn't bother him too much. He'd put on an extra shirt and wrapped a blanket over his shoulders. There wasn't much of a wind blowing to reach inside of the blanket. His toes, though. Even inside wool socks and heavy leather boots, his toes felt like they were frozen through.

They felt like icicles that would snap off with the slightest bit of pressure. Elias found himself idly thinking of a campfire. He was seeing in his mind the steps for building a campfire. Seeing the first lighting of the kindling. Seeing the growing orange flame spreading, licking at branches until it grew stronger, brighter, and warmer. He laughed quietly to himself as he realized he felt the tiniest bit warmer just thinking of a campfire.

Two days now since Zeke and the others had gone on ahead. Surely now they were down in the Umatilla Valley, outside of these mountains. It probably wasn't even snowing where they were. Maybe they were already arriving to the mission.

Elias and the others with the wagons now were lucky. They'd hit a long stretch of trail where there'd been no need to fell trees. Elias rode out ahead far enough that if he encountered a tight spot that needed to be cleared some, he could get the other wagons stopped in plenty of time. But since morning, they'd only once had to stop and take down a couple of trees.

As he rounded a bend in the trail, up ahead Elias saw some obstacle that made him frown. He couldn't figure it at first. About three to four feet high, covered in new snow. He clicked his tongue at Tuckee to speed up the horse. When he got to it, he saw that it was a pile of stacked rocks. Most of them were about the size of his boot, but they got smaller as the stack got higher so that the one on the top easily fit inside his fist.

It was a curious thing, a column of stacked rocks, until he realized that sticking out between two rocks near the bottom was a piece of fabric.

The stack of rocks would have to go, anyway, so Elias shook the blanket off his shoulders and laid it across Tuckee's rump, and then he swung himself down out of the saddle.

He picked up the top rock, a small stone that fit easily inside his palm. With his gloved thumb, he wiped the snow from it and then slid it down into his pocket. It felt cold and wet there against his leg, though that might have been his imagination, the same as his imagined campfire made him feel warmer.

Now he started removing rocks from the stack and tossing them into the woods. The bigger rocks near the bottom he had to lift with two hands and walk over to the edge of the trail and swing those in.

When he reached the cloth, he saw it was a silk kerchief. He recognized it. Silk with an edge of lace. Lavender flowers embroidered at the corners, and a lavender "MT" embroidered in the center.

Madeline Townes.

He recognized the kerchief, of course. He'd bought it for Madeline as a gift some years back.

"Everything okay?" Gabriel shouted ahead to his father as the wagon rounded the bend in the trail and Gabe saw his father standing in the trail and out of the saddle.

Elias waved the hand holding the handkerchief at his son.

"Everything's fine," he said. "Keep 'em rolling, Gabe."

Elias shoved the handkerchief down into his pocket with the stone.

THERE'D BEEN NO SNOW fall through the night. Just a clear, starlit night with the moon shining. Before turning in, Elias had spent some time looking at the moon and thinking that Maddie was not so far ahead of him, probably looking at it, too.

Elias woke feeling stiff and cold. In some of the wagons there was room for sleep. Whether on top of blankets piled on furniture or on dwindling sacks of flour. But most of the emigrants tried to find a way to sleep outside of the wagon – under it or inside a tent or at least on top of a blanket. The snow and mud made sleeping on the ground an unhappy proposition, but Elias and his sons and put down a blanket and slept on the ground.

"I think I had a rock under my back," Christian said.

"You should have moved it," Elias told him.

"It was too cold to get out from under the blankets."

"Uh-huh. Let's get up and get the day started," Elias told his son. "I'm hoping by the end of the day we'll be out of the mountains."

"At least it won't be snowing," Gabriel said. "It's a clear sky. I can see stars."

The first light of morning was beginning to shine in the early morning sky. Elias's shoulders and neck hurt. They'd finished the previous day by swinging axes, clearing a patch where the trail narrowed in front of them. Late in the day they'd come to the confluence of the creek they'd been following and another river. Tu Ah Tway had told him when they reached that river they'd be coming out of the mountains. Elias felt an excitement at the prospect that seemed to be shared among the other men still with the wagons. He could hear others down the wagon train up and moving early this morning. Probably no one slept well. Without tents and their wives, the last couple of nights had been plenty cold.

"I'll get the fire started and cook breakfast," Gabriel said.

"Christian and I will go and get the oxen."

Unable to circle the wagons on the narrow trail, they'd been constructing makeshift corrals by stringing ropes between trees to keep the livestock from wandering at night. It was hardly a necessary chore. The animals were hungry and exhausted. None of them would wander far at this point. Only a bear or some other predator would make them run now.

"What are the chances we'll be out of these mountains in this lifetime?" Jefferson Pilcher asked as Elias and Christian passed by his wagon.

"I hope good," Elias said. "From what the Natives told us, I think we might get clear of the mountains today."

"It would be nice," Pilcher said. "I don't fault you any for this, Elias. I know some of the others do. But I don't. All the same, I'm tired. I'm hungry all the time now. I'm just ready to get to a place and stay."

"It's been a long journey, Jeff. We're almost there."

"Have you thought about the Columbia?" Pilcher asked.

"It's all I'm thinking about," Elias confessed.

According to the book Elias used as his guide – and common knowledge of the trail – everyone knew that the Emigrant Trail ended at the Dalles. The journey to Oregon City required a raft at that point. Whatever people, animals, and supplies were going on to Oregon City would get there only by rafting the river. But Elias's pamphlet also said the river journey had to be made before October. Any later in the year and the river would be too high, too rough, for safe passage.

It was already October.

THE WIND CUT THROUGH the Umatilla Valley, pushing down the tall grass carpeting the bald, empty landscape.

The clouds had finally broken, the sun rose this morning, and a warmth and vitality swept across the land.

The Blue Mountains were behind them, sitting off their right shoulders and looking very small and insignificant. Zeke couldn't see the big peaks farther to the south, nor could he see from here just how high those mountains grew. From his current vantage, he could only see that first rise of the hills of the western slope, and at this distance it hardly even looked like a challenge. From here, it looked like a man could just drive a team of oxen and a wagon right up and over those hills in the distance.

It was their fourth morning since leaving the wagons. The night had been chilly but not terrible. Stars and moon bright in the dark sky. The day started cool and would likely remain so even when the sun was directly overhead, but with no protection from the sun, Zeke would be sweating soon enough.

"When I first met him in the forest, Tu Ah Tway told me that the mission was only two or three days away," Henry said, muttering under his breath to avoid being heard.

Zeke nodded his head.

"Well, it's day four today," Zeke said.

"You don't think he's leading us to an ambush, do you?"

Zeke gave a small shrug.

"I don't know, Henry. I don't think so. Tu Ah Tway and them other Injuns – Matthew, Mark, Luke, and John – they've been nothing but nice to us, and I'd hate to suspect them."

"Those aren't their names," Henry said.

"They're close," Zeke grinned at him. "I don't think the Christian names the missionaries call them are their names, either."

Henry shrugged.

"Maybe not."

"I don't think they're planning to ambush us," Zeke said. "That doesn't mean you should drop your guard, but I ain't too worried. Nevertheless, I'll go and have a word with Tu Ah Tway. Our provisions are running mighty short, and if we're going to be out here another day or two, we're going to need to do something."

The children had brightened considerably since coming out of the mountains. The snow had been a treat for them at first, but like their parents, they'd found the cold relentless. Now, running through the grass and chasing each other or laughing in the sunshine was the treat, even though that's how they'd spent almost every day of the last six months.

There were still a few campfires burning, though by now all the settlers had finished their breakfasts and were beginning to pack up their belongings to start the day again. The Indians had pitched in with the packing and loading the animals, and they were doing their part to keep the group moving. They weren't merely serving as guides, but they were helping in everything and in every way. Zeke figured more than a little of that Christian charity the missionaries had taught them had taken.

"I kind of figured we'd be to the mission by now," Zeke said to Tu Ah Tway.

"Huh," Tu Ah Tway said in a noncommittal sort of way.

Zeke had grown fond of their Indian escorts. Each evening, Tu Ah Tway came to Zeke's campfire and asked him about Jesus or asked him why he was traveling into Oregon Territory. Tu Ah Tway was very curious about everything, and Zeke soon realized that most of the Indian's conversations with white men had centered on Jesus. He'd almost exclusively been around missionaries, and Tu Ah Tway seemed surprised to encounter a white man who didn't want to read the Bible at him.

"Didn't you tell Henry that the mission was just a two day ride? It's the fourth day."

Tu Ah Tway gave a small shrug and glanced to the north, as if he could magically see the mission off in the distant horizon.

"We will get to the mission today," he said confidently. "These women and children move slower than Liksiyu riders."

"I imagine that's true," Zeke conceded.

"Today, Ezekiel," Tu Ah Tway promised. "We will be to the mission by nightfall."

The animals were revived.

They'd found plenty of good forage here in the Umatilla Valley. And because they were miles away from the trail, it wasn't all trampled under and eaten up by the thousands of horses and mules and oxen and cattle that had come to the Oregon Territory ahead of them.

"This is good land," Luke Suttle commented to Zeke. "I promise you, in twenty years this whole valley will be settled. This is one vast pasture just waiting for herds of cattle and teams of plows."

"Don't let Tu Ah Tway or his friends hear that prediction," Zeke said. "They're decent enough to us now, but I don't care to think how their attitudes might change if they thought too many more of us were coming."

Zeke whistled for his dogs to follow. His pack had grown significantly along this journey. Several of the other emigrant families brought at least one or two dogs along with them, but most of them had merged now into Zeke's group of dogs. Mustard and Towser led the pack, which worked well because they were the first two dogs to obey Zeke's whistle. When the emigrants started to move, a whistle or three got all of the dogs in the wagon train moving with them.

By mid-afternoon, the canyon had opened dramatically. The big hills closing them in had receded away. They'd come down out of the snow. The trees along the trail opened, and the emigrants found themselves outside of the forest and stretching out below them was the Umatilla Valley, glorious and golden, bathed in sunlight.

The wind blew constant and hard, but the sun came down just as persistently.

The men driving the cattle and the oxen abandoned their coats and blankets into their wagons, rolled up their sleeves, mopped their foreheads with bandannas.

"Hard to believe this time yesterday my teeth were chattering," Jerry Bennett said, riding up from the cow column to have a word with Elias.

"Amazing what a difference one day can make to the weather," Elias said.

"Well, a day and getting the hell out of those mountains," Jerry said. "What are your thoughts on stopping this afternoon?"

Elias nodded his head, agreeing with what he knew were Jerry's thoughts.

"Soon," he said, and as if to underscore the unspoken words between them, Tuckee stopped and tried to munch on the tall grass as they came into it. Elias had to pull the reins to get the horse's head back up. "Animals are hungry and have good forage for the first time in days. We'll make camp early this afternoon."

Jerry nodded his head.

"Thanks, Mr. Townes. It's about all we can do to keep the livestock moving," he said.

The men stopped soon after, circled their wagons and then turned out the animals, giving them free range to wander. None went far. A few of the horses trotted out to a hillside, but the oxen and cattle remained close to camp. They were still following the river as it came down out of the mountains, as Tu Ah Tway told them they should.

As the men made camp, Elias told Jeff Pilcher he thought this was the best camp they'd had since they were back near Bear River.

"We've got good grazing, fresh water, and plenty of willows and woody brush down along the riverbanks. It would be hard to ask for anything more."

"How do we find the Mission from here?" Pilcher asked.

"The Indians said we'll come to a creek that comes into the river from the north. Said at that creek we should head directly north and we'd come to the mission with no problem."

"I'm ready to get there," Pilcher said. "I never did like the idea of sending my wife and children off with those Indians."

Elias nodded. He understood.

"They'll be fine," he said. "Zeke's going to take care of the women and children. He won't let anything happen to them."

"I've got a lot of faith in your brother," he said. "If it had been anyone else, I'd have thought twice about letting my family go with them."

The two men stood awkwardly for several moments, and then Jeff Pilcher said, "I've got something else I want to ask you about, Elias. You probably can guess what it is."

"The Columbia River?" Elias said.

"That's right. Have you thought any more about it?"

Elias shook his head, not because he hadn't thought about it, but because he still didn't have an answer.

"Mr. Pilcher, my plan is to travel on to Oregon City," Elias said. "I intend to get there before the winter settles in. I don't know how I'll do it if the river is running too high or too rough to raft it, but I didn't come all this way to not make it to my destination."

"I agree," Pilcher said. "I have no interest in not getting where I'm going. But if I'm being honest about it, I don't know that I want to make a tough journey with some of these folks."

"I can understand that, too," Elias said.

"Would it be unreasonable to ask if you intend to break up the wagon train at The Dalles?"

Elias shrugged his shoulders.

"I don't know if I can do that. When these folks elected me to captain this wagon train – and I agreed – I took on a responsibility. It's like back at Bridger's Fort. I got everyone in the wagon train that far, where they were at least safe, and told them I was going on with my brother and they could come on or not. I reckon if folks still want to go on to Oregon City with me, they're welcome to do it. I won't tell anyone they can't."

"You'd be smart to tell Jeb Smith he isn't welcome with you," Pilcher said. "Maybe even tell him to form his own wagon train. It might weed out some of the less desirable families."

Elias nodded his head thoughtfully, though he didn't like talk of leaving folks behind or pushing them out. He agreed with what Jefferson Pilcher was saying. Pushing out Jeb Smith would be a good idea. Leaving behind some of the folks who didn't work as much, or complained a lot, or weren't particularly competent – nothing would do more to relieve some of Elias's worries. But he also couldn't betray the commitment he'd made as the captain of the wagon train. That wasn't the type of man that he was.

"We'll see when we get there," he said. "Right now, my priority is to get these wagons to the mission and then on to The Dalles."

9

TU AH TWAY AND one of the others of his hunting party rode some distance in advance of the emigrants, the others staying back to drive their six steers.

"I don't like the looks of that," Luke Suttle said, riding over to Zeke.

Zeke gave Duke a pat on the neck and shrugged his shoulders.

"I ain't overly worried, Mr. Suttle. I expect they're just scouting ahead to be sure of the way."

"Uh-huh. I hope so," Suttle said, doubtfully. "All these women, the livestock. If them Savages decided to meet up with some others and turn on us, we'd make for a mighty rich prize for them."

Zeke chuckled a bit.

"Mr. Suttle, they've been nothing but helpful to us."

"Which is exactly what they would be if they intended to do us harm. Lure us into a sense of comfort, then pounce on us."

Henry Blair was riding nearby, within earshot. Zeke laughed a little again and said, "You ain't got to worry about them pouncing, Mr. Suttle. We've got Henry Blair here. I reckon he could handle all six of these Indians and any friends they might scare up to help them. Henry did some Indian fighting when he was a trapper, you know."

"I'll keep my rifle close, all the same," Suttle said, and he turned his horse to ride back toward the livestock.

"That ain't true, Mr. Townes," Henry said. "When I was trapping out near Bridger's Fort, we got into a small scuffle with some Injuns. But I ain't never even fired my rifle. The others did, but I ain't never."

"I know it's not true, Henry," Zeke said. "I'm just trying to take some of the edge off Mr. Suttle's worry. You just ride along and do your part, and we'll be fine. These Indians don't mean us no harm. If they did, they'd have harmed us by now."

"How do you know that?" Henry asked.

"We've been at their mercy ever since we left my brother and the others. Yet Tu Ah Tway and his friends are having to help with the packing, they're having to drive the livestock, they're having to pitch in when we camp. If they meant to harm us, they'd have saved themselves all this work and done it a day or two ago."

Henry nodded his head.

"I guess that seems a reasonable assumption."

All the same, Zeke clicked his tongue at Duke and let the horse run ahead of the others. Mustard and Towser followed along, chasing through grass almost taller than them.

At the top of a hill, Zeke drew on the reins to bring Duke to a stop. Out ahead, about a mile or so away, ran a ribbon of trees, clearly indicating the presence of a creek or river. Zeke figured it must be a pretty good sized river by the amount of growth along it.

What he didn't see was what had happened to Tu Ah Tway and the other rider. But then, off to the west, he caught sight of them in the distance as they topped another hill. Zeke gave a tug, turning the horse to the left, and let him gallop down to the next hilltop. That's when Zeke saw what Tu Ah

Tway was looking for. Down near the river, another mile or so away, on a flat piece of ground, stood several buildings among cultivated fields. One of the buildings was very large.

They'd come to the mission.

Samuel Baxter stood well over six feet tall. Taller even than Zeke, who seldom found himself looking up at a man. Baxter wore his sideburns long down his cheeks and had a straw hat on his head, having been out in the fields.

He'd mounted a horse and ridden out with Tu Ah Tway to greet the emigrants. Even sitting in the saddle, his height was evident.

"Welcome," he said, riding up to meet Zeke who'd rejoined the others. Baxter extended his hand. "I'm Dr. Baxter."

"Zeke Townes."

"Adam tells me you've got wagons coming in a few days?"

"They're cutting a trail through the mountains," Zeke said. "We got turned around in the snow and lost the trail."

"Snow?" Baxter said, glancing to the east toward the Blue Mountains. "Has there already been snow?"

"A little," Zeke said. "If it's all right with you, we'd like to camp for a few days to wait for them."

"Oh, certainly!" Baxter said, and he seemed genuinely delighted at the prospect. "We didn't expect to see any more emigrants this late in the year. We had a wagon train pass through about a week and a half ago, and we were certain they would be the last."

"We've had some troubles," Zeke said.

Baxter surveyed the riders and animals coming behind Zeke.

"Mostly women?" he said.

"The rest of the men stayed with the wagons," Zeke said. "We'd found our way down to an old Indian hunting trail, from what Tu Ah Tway told us. Wide enough when we first got on it that we were confused, but hardly a trail the deeper along we got."

Baxter nodded his head as if he could understand, but Zeke wasn't sure that he did.

"The mountain forests can be confusing," he said.

"So we found ourselves having to clear trees away from the trail to get the wagons through," Zeke went on, somehow feeling like he owed the missionary an explanation. "I hope the others won't be more than three or four days behind us."

"However long it takes them, you're welcome here," Baxter said.

"The women can use the rest," Zeke went on. "It's been a difficult journey on all of us."

Baxter swept his eyes over the crowd of women. Most of them were mounted side-saddle, though a few preferred still to walk. Marie and Madeline and a few others sat astride their saddles, a scandalous behavior back east, but Baxter hardly seemed to notice.

"We have one pregnant woman, also," Zeke said. "She lost her husband along the trail and has three small children."

"Truly difficult circumstances, but I'm sorry to say not rare, either. What prospects does she have?"

"Her sister and her sister's husband are part of our party. Her mother, as well."

Baxter nodded.

"If she would prefer, we could make accommodations for her to stay on at the mission through the winter. She can have the baby here and make a decision what she wants to do in the spring. If she has family going on to the Willamette Valley, she can join them when conditions are better."

Zeke gave a glance over his shoulder at Sophie Bloom. She was still back a good distance, unaware that she was the topic of conversation. Currently she walked beside her horse, reins in her hand. All three of her children sat in the saddle as she led the horse.

"She might prefer that," Zeke said. "I know I'm obliged to you for making the offer."

"We have space here," Samuel Baxter said. "We couldn't house your entire company in our home, but we have room for a few. If you should decide to winter here, we can make accommodations."

Zeke nodded his head without committing one way or another.

"I know my brother is eager to reach Oregon City. But some of the others may choose to stay on through the winter."

Baxter smiled and cast another glance over the women and children, the first of whom now were reaching where the two men sat their horses talking.

"Well, those arrangements can be discussed later. Bring your people on to the mission. My wife, Narcissa, and I will be pleased to provide you some rest and comfort. You'll have plenty of time to tell me all about the troubles that have plagued you."

"YOUR BROTHER PAID THEM what?" Samuel Baxter asked, unable to hide his incredulity.

"Six steers," Zeke repeated.

"Huh," Baxter said, clearly contemptuous of such a price. "They'll butcher one tomorrow. Eat some of it and the rest will go rancid. The other five will wander off to be eaten by bear."

"Well, I think my brother decided that those steers were more of a burden to us and that we needed the help the Tu Ah Tway offered."

"Tu Ah? – Oh, you mean Adam. Yes, well, it was wasted generosity. They'll be back here stealing meat from me in a week. Of course, it was just as well that you paid them. The Natives have a queer concept of what's owed to them by white settlers. If you fail to pay them anything for using their land, they'll probably bash in your skull. I have an ongoing problem with the Cayuse who expect me to pay them for the property where the mission is. I think the only thing that has kept them from having at me is that I give them tobacco regularly."

The mission consisted of several buildings, among them a smithy and a grist mill. They had a farm of decent size with corn and other crops, most of them now harvested, and plenty of livestock. The main house was large with room for numerous guests. There were, as best as Zeke could figure, at least a dozen white men who had jobs around the farm.

After the livestock were turned out and tents erected and Zeke had seen to the needs of the women and children under his charge, he and Marie and Madeline, along with Captain Walker and his wife, joined Samuel and Narcissa Baxter for dinner in the mission's main house. It was the largest of the buildings at the mission, offering several guest rooms as well as a large room where Narcissa held English classes for the Natives.

"The hardest part is trying to make these Cayuse people understand me," Baxter complained over his glass of wine. "And I don't mean understand the language. Narcissa acts as a teacher here at the mission, and she has done a fine job of teaching the English language. But I mean getting them to truly understand me, and what I'm about. To understand my yearning to teach them about our Lord and Savior Jesus Christ. I want them to understand the grace of God and that I am here through His divine plan to bring His message of salvation to these savage people. But they will persist in praying to their ancestors and great spirits. They can't seem to grasp the concept of the Holy Trinity, three in one, or the grace that God extends to sinners through Christ's sacrifice. Mostly, they want to hear stories of Old Testament conquests. Joshua and David, Gideon and Samson."

"Do you find them to be friendly?" Marie asked.

"Friendly like wild dogs that you give food to," Narcissa answered. "You must be careful that they don't bite your fingers.

"Is that a foreign accent?" Baxter asked.

"My people were French and came up the river from New Orleans," Marie said. "I suppose I still carry a touch of their accents. My mother and father spoke French in the home."

"You carry more than a touch, I'd say. Please tell me you're not a Papist."

Marie shot a glance at Zeke.

"My parents are Catholics, and I was raised in the Catholic church. But Zeke grew up a Presbyterian, and we attended church together at the Presbyterian church in Paducah."

Baxter made a face of disgust.

"Presbyterians aren't all bad. At least you're moving in the right direction," Baxter said. Zeke thought the man was attempting to be charming, and he guessed that Baxter was likely smitten with Marie. Most men who encountered her became at least a little smitten with her. Zeke had grown accustomed to the way other men reacted to his wife, and it didn't bother him. But Marie shifted uncomfortably in her chair.

"We're low on provisions," Zeke said, drawing Baxter's attention back to him. "What prospects do we have to reprovision?"

Two Indian girls, wearing dresses that Narcissa must have given them, attended to the diners. None of the other people who worked at the mission joined them for dinner.

"Well, we have a station here at the mission for emigrants," Baxter said. "Ample stores of flour and corn meal. Preserves. Smoked meats, cheese. We also have a smithy if you need to make repairs to any of your wagons. And we won't gouge you on the prices the way some of the forts you passed might have. We consider our store for emigrants on the trail as part of the ministry we provide here. It's not just the souls of the Natives that we hope to save, but also we hope to offer God's succor to the travelers who pass by here."

"I'm grateful to hear it," Zeke said. "I know the others will be, as well."

"The Cayuse come and go at their will. They steal food when they're hungry, and we've had to whip some of them in the past. What frustrates me is that we treat them with generosity, but they still steal from us."

"They're not allowed in the main house," Narcissa said. "We have a door leading into the classroom from the outside, and that's as far as I will permit them to come into the house. When we first built the mission – six years ago, now – they came and went as they pleased. But they left every room absolutely filthy, tracking mud everywhere they went."

"Cayuse?" Zeke said. "They say they're Liksiyu People, but I've never heard of that tribe."

"You would know them as Cayuse. That's what the French-Canadian trappers called them, and that's what all the civilized people call them. They call themselves Liksiyu, but they understand that they are Cayuse."

"They're a dirty lot," Narcissa Baxter interjected again. "Absolutely filthy."

Baxter smiled at his wife.

"I'm afraid they made absolute pests of themselves when we first built the mission, and Narcissa doesn't care for them to enter the buildings."

"What about the sanctuary?" Madeline asked.

"Sanctuary? No, we have only a small chapel on the grounds of the mission. It isn't suitable for regular services for the Natives. We've held prayer meetings in the classroom, but usually when I hold services for the Cayuse we do so outside on the grounds."

"If you let the loose inside, they'll find something to steal."

"Are there hostilities with any of the Natives?" Captain Walker asked.

"Only scuffles from time-to-time," Baxter said. "Nothing that's ever amounted to much. They've held up some of the wagon trains near the Blue Mountains, demanding toll payments and claiming the wagons are crossing their lands. Usually, they can be paid off with a little tobacco. Though some of the trappers have paid them in guns and ammunition. I think that's dangerous business. Arming savages is a dangerous game, in my opinion. But the trappers, especially the French-Canadians and English-Canadians who came here years ago were careless about trade with the Natives."

"Those fellows who helped us here seemed all right to me," Zeke said.

"Adam and the others?" Baxter said. "They've been around the mission here for a long time. Ever since we built it, I guess. I have a very congenial relationship with Adam and some of the others, though their chief comes here every winter demanding payment for the mission's land. I've tried to explain to him that the mission's land was donated by the territorial governor, but he doesn't care for that answer."

"What does he want in the way of payment?" Zeke asked.

"Guns. Gunpowder. Tobacco. Livestock. Whatever I would be willing to give him, I suppose. But it doesn't matter, because I'll not pay. I've spent countless days trying to teach the Cayuse to farm, to cultivate the land. I've given them seeds and livestock. But they waste everything, they learn nothing, and then they steal from me."

Baxter laughed.

"I try to be forgiving," he went on. "It's what I'm called to do, after all. And how can I teach forgiveness without being forgiving myself? But I'm also trying to teach them respect for property, and that sometimes requires the whip."

"It's not easy to teach them," Narcissa said. "They are, after all, hardly smarter than beasts. I've seen skunks that were cleaner."

As dinner came to a close, the women exited into a parlor and the men went outside to smoke cigars and enjoy the cool evening air.

"Are there any notable people among your party, Mr. Townes?" Baxter asked. "Besides you and Captain Walker, of course? I ask because I like to offer a decent supper to anyone of note who passes by and stays at the mission for any length of time."

"I'm sure you'd enjoy having Marcus Weiss for supper," Zeke said. "He's with the wagons, now. But I'll certainly suggest you have supper with him when he arrives."

"Yes, that would be good," Baxter said. "Is he a Methodist?"

"I couldn't say, Mr. Baxter. But I think you'd enjoy the conversation."

"Ugh," Marie spat as she and Zeke entered their tent that night after being guests at the Baxter's dinner. "Those people are detestable."

Zeke laughed at her temper but did not argue with her.

"All that woman talked about was how dirty the Native people are," Marie went on. "They are supposed to be here ministering to them. And they call them dogs and beasts."

"Hello?" Madeline said from outside the tent, and Zeke opened the tent flap for her. Madeline stood there with a lantern in hand.

"Come on in," Zeke said.

Daniel was already asleep at one end of the tent. Marie and Zeke sat on the blanket they'd spread on the ground. The quarters were tight, but Madeline squeezed in and sat beside Marie.

"Please tell me I'm not alone in my opinion of our hosts," Maddie said.

"That's just what we were talking about," Marie said.

"It's a wonder the Cayuse Indians – or whatever they're called – have brained them with a hatchet," Maddie whispered.

"They certainly have a low opinion of the people they're purportedly here to help," Zeke agreed.

"I don't care what Elias says," Maddie went on. "I'll swim the Columbia River to Oregon City before I stay here for the winter."

"Elias isn't going to want any of us staying here for the winter," Zeke said. "I can promise you that."

"Those Indians were nothing but kind to us. They helped us the entire way and brought us here just like they said they would," Maddie said, fuming. "Their company was much more desirable than the company of the Baxters. I find their attitudes wholly objectionable."

Zeke grunted a little as Maddie's voice began to rise.

"The supplies they'll sell us will be the difference that gets us to Oregon City alive," he said.

"Perhaps, but it is a wonder to me that the Cayuse Indians, or whatever they're called, haven't done for that man and woman," Maddie said. "I do wish Elias would hurry. I want so desperately to be on our way. Why would the church send such uncaring people here to minister to the Natives?"

Zeke sighed and grinned at the anger of the two women.

"Perhaps the church leaders wanted to get the Baxters far away, and Oregon Territory was as far as they could get them."

"It would be no wonder," Marie said.

Over the next two days, the Baxters remained generous hosts, although Zeke privately cautioned everyone among their party to be careful how much generosity they accepted. He didn't know if Samuel and Narcissa Baxter were keeping a tally of every opened jar of preserves or every ear of corn and would present a statement of account before the emigrants departed.

For his part, Zeke engaged Samuel Baxter in conversation about everything from passage to Oregon City to the timber market in the territory, and Baxter was able to provide him with valuable information.

"The Columbia River should still be navigable now," Baxter said. "Your problem will be the backup of emigrants."

"How so?"

"From The Dalles to Oregon City, there is no route around Mount Hood and through the Cascade Mountains," Baxter explained. "Not for wagons, anyway. At The Dalles, you'll be forced to raft your wagons the remainder of the trip. There are men there who will get your wagons to Oregon City on a raft, but when you arrive you're going to find that the wagon trains in front of you are still waiting. There aren't enough men or rafts and too many emigrants. Everything is backed up at The Dalles. I would be very surprised if you found rafts available before the spring. Come winter, it will be too dangerous to get down the Columbia. The last I heard, they were charging forty dollars a wagon to raft them to Oregon City. It wouldn't surprise me if it's fifty dollars now."

"But there's a trail for the livestock?" Zeke questioned.

"Certainly. It's a trail that hugs the north face of Mount Hood and follows along beside the Columbia. But you cannot take wagons over that trail. It's too steep, too dangerous. The wagons have to go on the river. And some emigrants choose to sell their wagons and possessions and pack to Oregon City from The Dalles when they're confronted with the cost of a raft. Now, I did hear talk in the spring that a man was building a toll road south of Mount Hood. If that actually happened, if the road got built, I suppose that's a way you could get through. But I've been through the forest and mountains south of Mount Hood. I did it on horseback several years ago. I cannot imagine a road would be any better than the northern trail. No, Mr. Townes, I think you'd better resolve yourself to wintering at The Dalles and rafting your wagons in the spring."

As to the timber market, Baxter was very optimistic.

"This whole country is settling faster than you can imagine," he said. "In ten years, you won't be able to throw a stone in the Willamette Valley without striking some farmer on the head. I expect Oregon City to grow to be one of our finest cities on the Pacific Coast. You'll not be able to keep up with the demand for lumber if you hire a hundred or two hundred timbermen and build a dozen sawmills."

As to the Native population, Baxter considered them a lowly race and suggested it would be best if the government began removing them to agencies sooner rather than later.

"It will have to happen," he said. "And that it should happen before war breaks out would be best for all."

On the third day, Tu Ah Tway rode onto the mission, the first the emigrants had seen of him since he'd brought them here.

"Your wagons are close," he told Zeke. "We saw them about six miles from here."

The women and children greeted the news with great enthusiasm and rushed out onto the hills to greet them. They took picnics and blankets and made an afternoon of it, waiting for the wagons to appear on the horizon. But six miles in wagons drawn by weary animals can be a grueling six miles, especially considering that Zeke and the other men drove many of the spare oxen on ahead with them. The beasts pulling the wagons were overworked and even the sunshine and good forage had not restored them completely. It was nearly dusk when at last the wagons appeared, and by then most of the women had given up and returned to their tents at the mission.

10

THE TROUBLE STARTED ON the eve of the third day, and Beth Gordon started the trouble.

Elias had made it plain to everyone in the party that he intended to drive on for Oregon City, but that those who wished to should remain at the Baxter Mission for the winter. He'd made emphatic hints at Jeb Smith and Marcus Weiss that they should consider staying on at the mission. He talked to Wiser and Solomon McKinney about Sophie Bloom.

Sophie's sister Abigail was married to Solomon McKinney, and as such the McKinney brothers had taken some responsibility for Sophie since the death of her husband. But they'd also had to take responsibility for Betty Carlisle, who was Abigail and Sophie's mother. The burden of the pregnant Sophie Bloom, her children, and his mother-in-law had been more than Solomon had bargained for.

But Sophie Bloom said she intended to go on.

"I can't bear to be separated from the only family I have," she said.

Elias's frustrations grew over the course of the day, and he began urging everyone in the party to winter at the Baxter Mission. He said it was too late in the season to build a cabin before winter was upon them. There would be few, if any, rooms to let at Oregon City. The winter here would be milder than on the west side of the Cascade Mountains – this bit of information came from Samuel Baxter, and Elias did not know if it was true, but he said it like it was the gospel.

"I don't know what the next portion of this journey is going to look like, but I can guarantee it will be arduous," Elias said to every man in the wagon train.

Later, he confided to Zeke.

"The truth is, I don't want any of them to come," Elias told his brother. "They exhaust me with their petty bickering and their constant complaints. I just want to get to Oregon City and get to work. You and me and our hired men. That's all I want to be responsible for."

After supper that evening, with most everyone vowing to keep going and the rest at least making some noise in that direction, a couple of the men built up a large bonfire, and the entirety of the Townes Party, women and children included, came together for a meeting.

"I promised to get you to Oregon City," Elias said. "And if you choose to move out with me in the morning, I'll make good my promise. But I think the next few months will be hardship on anyone who continues going. It's so late in the season that we can expect little in the way of assistance when we arrive in Oregon City. Reverend Baxter says there is a road, but it may be that we'll have to build our own rafts and maneuver them ourselves down the Columbia River. I don't know if everyone here is prepared for that. And I think it might be best for some of you to consider staying on here. If you choose to stay, I'll refund what remains of the money you paid to buy into the wagon train."

Captain Walker adamantly refused to stay behind and was the first to speak up.

"I'm bound for Oregon City, and that's where I intend to go," he said.

"My vote is to go on with Mr. Townes," Jefferson Pilcher said. "Elias has gotten us this far, and I trust him to get us the rest of the way."

And that's when Beth Gordon decided to speak. Her gossip had been the source of plenty of trouble all the way back to the Missouri River.

"Maybe Mr. Townes should be replaced as the captain of the wagon train," she said.

"Huh," Zeke grunted, loud enough for Elias and several others to hear.

"Jeb Smith could lead this wagon train just as well as Mr. Townes," Marcus Weiss spoke up.

Elias was standing near the bonfire where the light hit him. The emigrants stood in a large half circle around him with Zeke and a few others standing off behind Elias. Now, Jeb Smith walked out of the crowd and turned to face the others, standing directly in front of Elias. A murmuring had started among the people, and Smith raised up his hands to try to silence the crowd.

"Let me say this, first of all," Smith started. "We only joined this wagon train at Bridger's Fort, so I don't have the advantage of having known all of you all the way back since Missouri. "But I'm troubled by much of what I've seen since Bridger's. Mr. Townes hired a gang of outlaws to guide us. They killed the Barnes girl and Mr. Long, and for all we know they might have done the same to Reverend Marsh and his wife. Mr. Townes got us lost in the Blue Mountains, and if we'd not come across friendly Savages, we might well have froze to death."

"The trail we were on led us directly out of the mountains and straight to the mission," Jefferson Pilcher said. "Nobody was going to freeze to death."

"Maybe," Jeb Smith said. "Maybe so. All we know for sure is that we had to rely on friendly Savages to get us here."

"It's time for someone new to lead this wagon train!" a woman shouted from the crowd, and Elias felt certain it was Beth Gordon's voice he recognized.

"I'll get you to Oregon City," Jeb Smith said. "Just as importantly, I'll get your property to Oregon City. That is a promise Mr. Townes can't keep, as I'm all too aware."

Zeke watched his brother's face as the light of the flames danced across it. He could see Elias's consternation and understood the battle raging within him. Elias had taken on the responsibility of the wagon train, and he was a man who possessed a strong sense of duty. At the same time, he'd become weary of those in his charge. He'd like nothing more than to see the emigrants go on with Jeb Smith. But Elias also had a low opinion of Smith. He thought the man's temper could be dangerous.

"Look here," Zeke said, stepping forward. "We're rolling out in the morning. Anyone who chooses to go with us can come. Anyone who chooses to stay here can stay. Reverend Baxter has made that offer. And if you want to go with Mr. Smith, you're welcome to that, too. If you want your money back for what's left of the journey, you'd better come see us soon. We'll be turning in soon enough to rest in advance of leaving in the morning, and we won't be settling accounts tomorrow."

"Thieves!" Jeb Smith shouted.

Zeke grabbed him by the collar and spun him around, ready to throw a fist, but he felt Elias's arms wrap him up and pull him back.

"None of that, Zeke," Elias whispered at his brother.

"Mr. Page, might I have a word with you?"

Jerry Bennett whistled and grinned. Caleb Driscoll and Will Page, Cody's brother, both giggled like a couple of children, and Cody glared at the three of them.

"Of course, Miss Bloom," Cody said. "You boys go on ahead. I'll catch up."

The hired men who'd been running the cow column had been camping on the outskirts of the mission, staying close to their animals. The other men walked on now and left Cody and Sophie Bloom standing in the firelight.

"You've been so kind to me since Mr. Bloom's death," Sophie said, looking at the ground.

"It ain't kindness," Cody said in humility. "Mr. Townes asked me to drive your wagon, and since he pays my wages, I do as I'm told."

Sophie glanced up to him now, wondering if she'd misread their relationship. Cody saw the concern on her face, and tried to correct himself.

"Sorry, ma'am. Maybe I should have said that different. What I mean is, I'm happy to help you. I appreciate the meals you've cooked for me, and I've enjoyed your company. I'm glad to drive your wagon."

"Mr. Townes makes a compelling argument that I should stay here. Pregnant, as I am, and with a difficult journey ahead."

"Yes, ma'am," Cody said. "It could be pretty tough going beyond The Dalles. I ain't for certain what we're in for."

"And I don't have any prospects in Oregon City. Whatever I do, I can only expect to be a burden on someone. Either I burden the Baxters or I burden my brother-in-law."

"Oh, I don't think you'd be a burden, ma'am. I don't think Mr. McKinney views you that way, and you shouldn't view yourself that way."

"A pregnant woman with three children already and my husband deceased? About my only prospects are to be a burden on someone."

"You're a fine cook, Miss Bloom. And a handsome woman, if you don't mind me saying so."

"I wonder how much of an imposition I would be on your kindness if I decided to disregard Mr. Townes's advice and continue on to Oregon City."

Cody smiled at her.

"It ain't no imposition, Miss Bloom. I'm going there anyway. Whether I go driving your wagon or riding a horse and pushing them steers, I'm going to Oregon City. I might as well take you along."

"You're sure?" Sophie Bloom asked.

"I am sure, ma'am. And as far as your prospects in Oregon City go, maybe there's more than you'd think. I know I'm just a tree man, but Mr. Townes is generous with his wages. And him and Zeke are smart men about business. I could see a time when I might be foreman of a crew, and Mr. Elias, he'd pay me right well. Enough to keep a family on. If I ain't being too forward, all I'm trying to say is that I'd like you to think of me as a prospect."

"You're a very decent man, Mr. Page."

"WE'RE CASHING OUT, MR. Townes," Luke Suttle said. He had Walter Brown with him.

Madeline consulted the ledger book to see what the Suttles and Browns had paid to join the wagon train. Like Jeb Smith, the Suttles and Browns had been in another wagon train as far as Bridger's Fort. There, or somewhere along the way, the three families had decided to make for Oregon instead of California, and they'd left their original wagon train and joined with the Townes Party. As such, they didn't spend as much to buy in as all the others, and they got less back.

"I want you to know, Mr. Townes, it's no reflection on you nor any objection to your leadership," Brown said. "But we've been with Mr. Smith since we come across the Missouri, and Mr. Suttle and I both felt we should stick with him."

"No hard feelings, Mr. Brown," Elias said.

"None of what's happened was your fault," Suttle kicked in. "You hired the only men available at Bridger's, and nobody can fault you for what they did. And losing the trail back in the mountains? Hell, I don't remember Jeb nor Hezekiah saying we was on the wrong trail. But like Walt said, we been with Jeb and Hezekiah from the start and feel we owe it to him."

"I understand," Elias said. "When we meet in Oregon City, it'll be as friends."

Marcus Weiss was next to cash out, and he did it with less apology.

"I have nothing against you, Mr. Townes, but your brother is a danger-ous man, and a murderer, and I've objected to his presence since he killed my driver. I intend to throw in with Jeb Smith."

Elias bit his tongue and offered nothing but a civil response back. He'd have liked very much to offer Weiss a punch in the nose, but refrained from that, too.

A couple of the packers who'd been with them since the Missouri River also came by Elias's tent. Hugh Anderson and Jack Horne had helped to drive the livestock and their pay had been the protection of the wagon train, free meals along the trail, and they didn't have to buy in the way the other families did. They didn't come to collect money, but to explain.

"Mr. Smith offered us wages to drive livestock," Anderson said. "If you want to offer us pay, we'll stay with you."

"That's okay, boys. It's been good traveling with you, and if you find yourselves in Oregon City looking for work, feel free to come and find me. I expect we'll need hands at the sawmill."

Anderson seemed genuinely regretful about leaving, and Elias was sorry to see him go. He'd been a solid hand the whole way. A hard worker. Elias was serious about the offer for work in Oregon City. Horne wasn't quite the worker that Anderson was, but Elias would hire him, too, if he turned up in Oregon City.

John Gordon turned up looking to cash out, and Elias wasn't sorry to see him go. Gordon was all right, but his wife Beth was a constant source of irritation, a complainer who'd soured the well with her constant gossip.

When it was all done, eleven families and two packers chose to join Jeb Smith.

He also hired half a dozen Cayuse who were there at the mission to drive livestock and help with the wagons. The Cayuse each had at least enough English to communicate with the settlers.

"We started with thirty-six wagons," Elias said to Madeline. "We had four families go back before we ever got to the Platte River. We brought thirty-two wagons into Bridger's Fort, and picked up three more. We lost one on the Snake River and one in the Blue Mountains. And now we've lost eleven wagons. If we make it to Oregon City, we'll have twenty-two of the wagons we started with. I'd say that's pretty poor."

"Oh, don't be like that, Elias," Madeline said. "Good riddance to all of them. It would be worth it to see the entire wagon train except for our immediate family and friends leave off just to get rid of Jeb Smith and his father and Marcus Weiss and that terrible woman Beth Gordon. We should be dancing for joy at our good fortune."

11

To anyone who might have viewed them from a distance, the two small wagon trains would have looked absurd cutting out from the Baxter Mission. An onlooker with no knowledge of what had transpired would easily see how they deliberately avoided each other yet followed the same path.

That first day, they traveled within sight of each other, the train led by Jeb Smith following with about a mile's distance between him and the wagons led by Elias Townes.

When Elias called for a halt late in the afternoon, the Smith Party veered around the circled wagons and kept going. The broke for camp about two miles beyond where the Townes Party camped.

"We should hitch our teams and move ahead of them," Zeke said to Elias.

"No reason to be petty," Elias said.

"I ain't being petty," Zeke said. "I'm thinking about The Dalles. We don't want one more wagon train in front of us to wait that much longer for rafts to haul the wagons ahead."

"If what Baxter told us is true, I don't think we'll be rafting down the Columbia River," Elias said. "If there's a road open to Oregon City, we'll take that."

"You think a road would be faster?"

"I think the wait in The Dalles will keep us there until springtime. If we take the road, we're in charge of what happens to us and when. If we go the river, we're waiting on someone else. And that's assuming anyone is even still running rafts down the river."

Zeke grunted.

"I still don't think I want them in front of us," he said.

Baxter said it would likely take five or six days to reach The Dalles more than eighty miles from the mission, and Elias announced that he wasn't inclined to push hard.

"If there's a road to Oregon City from The Dalles, we know it will be rough," Elias predicted. "Probably the toughest part of the journey we've encountered. I won't drive the animals too hard now knowing that's in front of us."

The second day out, the Townes Party lost sight of Smith and his group. They rose and moved out before sunup.

"He's racing us to The Dalles to prove he can beat you," Wiser McKinney told Elias. "But no one who stayed with you considers this a race. You're being smart to spare the animals."

The third day out, Henry Blair was scouting ahead. The wagon train meandered down in a flat space between big, rolling hills. They were back on the Oregon Trail, now – and had been since arriving at Baxter's Mission – following along the well-worn path used by the wagon trains that had come before them. There wasn't much real necessity of scouting ahead. Henry wasn't trying to keep the wagon train on the trail. All he really did was look for obstacles along the trail or danger from wild animals. Grizzly and such were here, and they were following along close to the Columbia River, now, which increased the likelihood of encountering bear near the water.

But when Henry came riding back at a gallop toward the wagon train, it wasn't bear he'd seen.

"Mr. Townes!" Henry shouted, his reins in one hand and his other hand holding his hat on his head. "You've got to come see this!"

Elias didn't ask questions, expecting the worst. He quickly saddled his horse and followed Henry Blair. Henry led him along the trail, down below the hills for about a mile, and he rode up one of the big rolling hills. There, at the top, Henry reined in. He turned and watched Elias as he came up behind Henry.

"Oh, my," Elias breathed. He'd never seen anything like it. He felt his head swim at the enormity.

He couldn't judge the distance – couldn't even fathom it. Off on the horizon, between the rolling greenish-brown hills of billowing rye grass, Elias saw a strip between land and sky of blue-gray mountains, and right in the center of it, framed perfectly between two nearby hills, a monstrous cone rising to tower over that line of mountains. At first, Elias's eyes told him it must be clouds he saw, but there were no other clouds in the clear blue sky. It was snow covering half the distance from the wide base to the narrow top.

"That's Mount Hood," Elias said, his voice husky and full of wonder.

"Ain't it amazing?" Henry asked. "I just sat here staring at it. Then I had to come back and get you."

"Unbelievable," Elias said. "My head is swimming. I feel like I could fall down right out of this saddle."

Somehow – Elias couldn't explain it – his mind seemed unwilling or unable to accept the overwhelming size of the mountain. He felt as if he was looking down on it, rather than looking up at it, and for a moment he thought he might fall to the ground.

"It's gorgeous," Henry said.

The two of them sat for a moment, contemplating the enormity of the mountain before them. Elias began to wonder how they would even be able to go around it, and for the first time since he'd picked up the pamphlet he used as a guide for the Oregon Trail, he realized exactly why emigrants used the Columbia River to reach the Willamette Valley.

"We're going to have a helluva time getting to the other side of the mountain," Elias said.

They stopped the wagon train and made camp at the foot of the hill even though it was early in the afternoon and they could have gone on for another hour or so.

After consulting his map and brochure, Elias decided they had to be about fifty miles from the mountain.

"I thought it was something everyone should see, and really be able to fix in their minds," Elias told Zeke later when his brother questioned why they didn't press on. "I expect most of us will only make this journey once in our lives, and wanted everyone to be able to remember the first time they saw Mount Hood."

"Big as it is, I expect we'll spend every morning for the rest of our lives living in its shadow," Zeke said.

"Probably so," Elias laughed. "But nothing will ever replace the memory of the first time we saw Mount Hood."

"No, sir. No more rafts are going to Oregon City until late spring. We've got four wagon trains in front of you, and we've promised those folks we'll take them if the rains don't start and the water don't rise too much. But we'll be lucky to get two of them wagon trains to Oregon City."

Elias nodded at the man and glanced at Zeke. They'd already decided they would be unwilling to offer a higher price to jump ahead in the line. They'd almost surely find themselves in a bidding war that might leave them worse off for winning it.

"I hear there's a road around Mount Hood," Zeke said. "Do you know about that?"

The man wore a sailor's cap which seemed fitting for the captain of the fleet of rafts transporting wagons down the Columbia River. But he was a big man around the middle, and Zeke didn't think he'd ever been on a ship. Big men couldn't climb riggings, and the ship mess didn't feed folks enough to get them so large. This was a man who'd spent his life achieving his present state of girth.

"Huh? A road? Why, a man would be a fool to try to build a road through the Cascade Mountains. That river right there is the only road, and until next spring – as far as you're concerned – it's closed."

They'd arrived at The Dalles the previous afternoon and made camp outside the town.

Elias had expected a settlement of some size. He knew the place had started as a gathering spot for Natives and fur trappers. Then it housed a mission. He'd heard that emigrants found lodging here and expected a town reminiscent of those back on the banks of the Missouri. Instead, just a handful of buildings made up the town center. Two of those buildings were crowded saloons on either side of a brewery; the hardware store had almost nothing to sell, and the dry goods store was almost just as empty. Sugar, flour, coffee, and corn meal were all in short supply, though beans and rice – staples in any wagon train – were plentiful. The butcher had fresh meat and smoked meat, but the Townes Party didn't lack for meat.

"It's a good thing we reprovisioned at Baxter's mission," Zeke commented-ed when he and Elias and Jefferson Pilcher went to the town to see about hiring rafts to move the wagons down the Columbia.

The town, what there was of it, was built into the bluffs overlooking the river. There were several small cabins scattered around the commercial buildings, and Elias got the impression there were more cabins built further up away from the river.

They found the raft man in a log cabin near the river that served as both his home and his place of business. His name was Richard Morgan, and everyone in The Dalles, whether a local who lived and worked here or an emigrant who just rode up in a wagon train, knew where to find him.

He'd been pretty curt about it, explaining that he wouldn't be able to load their wagons on a raft until next year.

"What about building our own rafts?" Zeke asked him.

"I can't stop you," Morgan said. "Some do. I would advise against it. My boys know this river and they'll take your wagons to Oregon City the fastest, safest way possible. But if you want to try it yourself, I wouldn't try to stop you."

"We come from Kentucky," Zeke said. "Floated plenty of rafts down the Ohio."

Morgan laughed.

"I used to work a riverboat on the Mississippi. I know the Ohio River. The Columbia River ain't no Ohio River, I'll tell you that. The banks of the gorge are steep. You're talking about eighty miles of choppy water. Whole stretches, you won't find a place to beach your raft. There's rocks, and you'll see them coming at you, and you'll think you're just fine. But the river moves so fast, and next thing you know, your raft is smashed all to bits and you're swimming in that freezing cold water."

Richard Morgan looked over the three men.

"Everyone in your party know how to swim?"

"Not everyone," Elias said.

"Well, I won't say nothing to try to talk you out of it, but you wouldn't be the first men to try this river on your own. Most of them, like yourselves, have been on some of them rivers back East. The Ohio. The Mississippi. The Missouri. But this one ain't none of those. The smart ones hire my boys to run the river for them. Almost all of my men are Indians. They raft this river in their bare feet."

"Well, Mr. Morgan, I appreciate your advice," Elias said. "We'll have to talk about what we're going to do, but I suspect there's a good chance we'll be back to see you."

"Don't wait too long," Morgan said. "I run a first come, first served business here, but you ain't got a place in line until you make your deposit. As it stands now, you'll already be my second or third wagon train for next spring."

The Townes brothers and Jefferson Pilcher left Morgan's house, all of them silent until they'd gotten some distance away.

"For a man who says he ain't going to try to talk us out of rafting these wagons ourselves, he sure did have a lot of words to say against it," Zeke chuckled.

"Let's find someone who knows about the road," Elias said.

105

"You go south from here, a day and a half through the Tygh Valley. You pick up the road there. It's a toll road. Five dollars a wagon, ten cents a head of livestock."

The man they found who knew of the Barlow Road was one of two blacksmiths in town. After leaving Richard Morgan, the three men made their way back to their camp where they got two wagon wheels that needed repairs. They brought the wagon wheels to the blacksmith and when they asked about the Barlow Road, he said he knew of it.

"How is the road?" Elias asked.

"I couldn't say," the blacksmith shrugged. "Ain't never been on it. Man named Barlow built it. Finished it this year. He come up with a wagon train last year, and like yourselves found himself at the back of a long line of folks waiting for passage down the Columbia River. Him and some others forced their way through the forest, going around the south side of Mount Hood. They done that last year. Then he got permission from the territorial government to build the road, and they worked on it for months."

"Have other wagon trains taken the road?" Elias asked.

"A few that I know of. But most prefer to wait for the rafts. I think folks don't know about the road, yet. It ain't been finished but a couple months ago."

"And the wagon trains that took the road, did they make it to the other side? Are they in Oregon City now?"

The blacksmith scratched at his head.

"I couldn't say for sure," he said. "I ain't heard of no lost or stranded settlers, if that's what you're worried about. But if they made it, I don't know."

"Would you take the road or wait for the rafts?"

The smithy laughed.

"I wouldn't do neither," he said. "I come up here ten years ago with some trappers. Worked at Fort Vancouver for some time, then come here about five years ago. I done all the traveling I care to do. If I live out my days and never go more than ten miles from this spot, I'll have gone too far."

"Right," Elias said. "But if you had to go, which route would you prefer?"

"I'd go by water. Get yourself up on a hill somewhere and take a look at that mountain to the south. Look at how big it is, and imagine for yourself the sorts of gorges and canyons and cliffs you'd have to navigate to get around the thing. I can't believe any road that I would want to travel on can be made across that mountain."

"Is there a guide we can hire to take us to the road?" Elias asked.

The smithy thought about it a moment.

"Harrison Locke was here at The Dalles a couple of weeks ago. He helped to build the road. But he's moved on, I think. He'd be your best guide. Oh! You know what? There's a halfbreed Injun, the son of a French-Canadian trapper. His name is Renard. Renard hired on to help build that road. You go down to the saloon, you'll find him there. He won't be sober, but he'll be able to get you to the road. Once you're on it, you won't need a guide."

"Is he trustworthy?" Jeff Pilcher asked.

The smithy laughed.

"He ain't. No. But neither is any other man who would take you. He'll steal whatever he can from you. And he'll drink. But you pay him five dollars, and he'll get you down through the Tygh Valley to the start of the road."

Outside the smithy's shop, rain had started to fall. A light shower had started and seemed unlikely to quit anytime soon, and dusk was upon them. Zeke pulled his coat tight at the neck and held it there, wishing he'd brought a warmer coat.

"Where to now? The saloon?"

"I reckon so," Elias said. "Unless you know where the Tygh Valley happens to be located."

"I don't," Zeke grinned.

"It ain't in my book, neither."

The saloon was crowded largely with what the emigrants took to be their fellow travelers. Three men worked behind the bar, and Elias, Zeke, and Pilcher had to push past the crowd to get up to the bar.

"We're looking for a man called Renard," Elias said to the barkeeper.

"Renard?" the man laughed. "He's a popular figure tonight."

The barkeeper craned his neck, looking around. His eyes fell on a small crowd up against the far wall.

"You'll find Renard behind those men there."

Elias looked in the direction the bartender indicated. He didn't see Renard, but he recognized the men standing in front of him: Jeb Smith, Marcus Weiss, and Luke Suttle. And then Elias saw Hezekiah Smith pushing past the crowd toward him.

"Hard luck, Mr. Townes," the elderly man said. "We come to him first. Looks like you're still a step behind."

12

"WE'RE GOING TO FEEL pretty foolish if that fellow Renard doesn't know the way," Zeke muttered to Henry Blair.

Henry laughed.

"At least we ain't pay him nothing," Henry said.

Elias frowned at the two of them.

"Follow Smith and them others," Elias said. "Find the way. We'll start out tomorrow, when the stock is rested and the wheels are mended and we've got supplies enough to get us to Oregon City."

"So you'll be just a day behind us?" Zeke said.

When they'd gotten back to camp after their failed effort to hire a guide, Elias brought Zeke, Henry, and Billy Tucker together.

"That's right. The day after tomorrow, you send Billy back to guide us. He can meet us however far we get without a guide. The next day, you send Henry back. And when you've laid eyes on the road and you know the way to the tollgate on the Barlow Road, you ride back and lead us the rest of the way."

Zeke squinted at his brother.

"This feels dishonest," Zeke said. "Are we doing something dishonest here?"

Elias sighed and shrugged.

"Honestly, Zeke? I don't know if it is or not. We've followed the path of wagon trains this far. Some, or maybe all, of those had hired captains who knew the way. This ain't no different."

"All the same, we should probably stay out of sight?" Zeke said.

Elias nodded his head.

"You should probably stay out of sight. There's a good chance Jeb Smith and Marcus Weiss might think there's something dishonest about us following them."

The Smith Party rolled out of The Dalles the next morning. The Townes Party watched them start out for the Tygh Valley. And then Zeke, Henry Blair, and Billy Thomas mounted their horses and followed some distance behind.

The route to the Tygh Valley took the emigrants back to the east a couple of miles before they turned south over rolling hills covered in bunch grass that seemed perpetually pushed down by the strong winds that blew over the hills. Much of the way, the emigrants had a view of Mount Hood off their right shoulders.

The three riders stayed back from Smith's wagon train, out of sight, and the surrounding hills made that a simple task. In places, they could be within a few hundred yards of the wagon train, close enough that they could hear children and barking dogs and lowing cattle, and still not be within sight.

Their second morning out, Billy Tucker turned back north to meet up with Elias and the wagon train and lead them in the right direction.

The next morning, Zeke sent Henry Blair back to guide the wagon train to the canyon, and as Henry headed back north, Zeke continued to follow Smith's wagon train.

On the fourth day out from The Dalles, the Smith Party started the morning in a canyon between high hills and by midday had dropped down into a valley. Following behind, alone now, Zeke assumed they were entering the Tygh Valley.

In the afternoon, the wagons arrived at a farm where they stopped to make camp. At first, Zeke thought they were just calling an early halt to their travel. But staying out of sight, he watched as the farmer approached the wagons from his home. There was a lengthy discussion, and then the man returned to the house. Then, looking over the place, Zeke saw a bridge crossing a heavily wooded creek beyond the house. There was a gate in front of the bridge. This was it, Zeke realized: The tollgate on the Barlow Road.

Having seen the gate, Zeke returned to his horse. He gave Duke a pat on the neck.

"We might as well turn back from here. Once they're beyond the gatehouse, we won't need them to follow the road. They've shown us the way this far, and that's all we needed them to do."

Zeke thought they probably could have arrived at the tollgate without following Smith's wagon train, even without a guide. The trail from The Dalles to the beginning of the road was pretty easy to follow. It tracked along with the natural contour of the land, crossing hills and dropping into canyons. And though the trail wasn't as worn as the Emigrant Trail, enough wagons had come this way in recent weeks that a man didn't have to look hard to see where the wagons had traveled.

As he turned Duke back to the north, Zeke was eager to get back to Marie and Daniel.

Elias called a halt to the day's travel on a wide hilltop with a spectacular view of Mount Hood to the west.

A stiff wind pestered the emigrants as they made their camp for the evening, harassing them as they built their campfires and tried to put up their tents, but the forage here was good, and there was a creek down below them that provided them with water, and they didn't have to worry about the stock wandering from here.

Madeline made dinner over the campfire, building it down near the wagon in the hopes that the wagon would help to break the wind.

Elias and the other men turned out the livestock and collected water from the creek down below them to wash the oxen and horses.

With the weather getting cold at night, the children collected bunch grass to lay over the backs of the wet animals, and then the older boys and their fathers blanketed the animals. It was a new end-of-the-day chore that had caused much complaint among the younger children.

With their work done, the men and boys returned to their wagons, hoping their suppers would be ready.

Madeline laughed as she ate, her eyes on Mount Hood in the distance. Elias looked up at her, noticing the lack of humor in her laugh.

"What's funny?"

"I was just thinking, up on this hill with that wind blowing and feeling cold like I am, it seems so far away."

"What seems so far away?" Elias asked.

Maddie nodded her head toward the mountain and Elias twisted to see it. He held a plate in his hands with beans and rice and a thick gravy Maddie had made. He mixed the beans in with the rice and gravy.

"The mountain," Maddie said. "It seems so far away, and I keep telling myself that home is just on the other side of that mountain. But nothing here feels like home. It feels cold and distant. I tell myself we're almost home, but I can't believe it. Honestly, Elias, this hilltop feels more like home. This wagon feels more like home than anything on the other side of that mountain."

Elias nodded his head thoughtfully.

"When we get there," he said. "It will feel like home when we're there. Our children will be there. You and I will be there. Zeke and Marie. It will feel like home. And if it doesn't, when we get the cabin built, we'll park this old wagon outside the front door and then you'll always be home."

Maddie laughed, this time with a little more humor.

"I believe the wagon might help," Madeline said. She breathed a heavy sigh and stood up, her plate in her hand. "And yes, I know you're right. Our children will be with us. Thank God Maggie and Jason made the trip with us. I don't know if I could bear it if they were back in Kentucky. I'll be fine, Elias. I think the chill and the desolation of this place is getting to me."

Elias looked around. The place did feel pretty desolate. It was overcast today, though there'd been no rain. The wind swept across the land. The hills were bare of trees. All the trees within sight were down in the hollers by the creek. In every way, today felt like a cold winter's day.

"Everything will be fine, Maddie," Elias said. "We talked about this for months. We've planned it. We're certain we're doing the right thing for our family. When we get to the other side of that mountain, we'll make it our home no matter what it takes."

Maddie nodded her head.

"I'll be fine tomorrow," she said. "I'll change my thinking about it and be excited again. Just today I'm feeling a little emotional."

Elias reached out and patted her leg.

"I understand," he said.

But in truth, Elias later confessed to Wiser and Solomon McKinney that he didn't understand.

"I feel like I have bees buzzing inside me," Elias said. "When I look out at that mountain and realize that's all that stands between me and my new life, I cannot hardly contain my excitement."

"You have every reason to feel excited, Elias," Solomon said. "And she has every reason to feel trepidation. Both points of view are forgivable."

"What about you?" Elias asked. "How do you feel?"

"Oh, I'm excited as well," Solomon said. "Though I'm also nervous. For us, the winter means building our cabins as quickly as possible so that come spring we can begin planting."

"It's going to be a busy time," Wiser agreed. "We'll work twice as hard in the next eight to ten months as we've ever worked."

As the three men continued to talk, the conversation went around to Jeb Smith and his group. The animosity among Smith and his people seemed absurd to Elias. The McKinney brothers shared Elias's assessment.

"There's no need for it," Wiser said. "The incident with the wagon – that was an accident for which you bore no responsibility."

"He's an envious man," Solomon said. "I smelled it on him the moment I met him back at Bridger's Fort. He's the sort of man who sees what others have, and he wants it for himself. He saw you leading the wagon train, and he wanted to be the man leading the wagon train. He was envious of your position and took advantage of his own misfortune to try to steal that position from you. Personally, I worry that they'll come to disaster."

"It won't be that," Elias said. "It's not that difficult to tell people to get their wagons rolling and to tell people to stop and make camp. That's about all I've had to do."

"Oh, I don't think that's true," Solomon said back. "I think you've done a great deal more than that to get all of us this far. And I think the only thing that will save Jeb Smith from bringing himself or some of those others to ruin will be the shortness of the journey they have left. If he was starting from the Missouri River, he'd surely lead them to some terrible tragedy. But because we're a hundred miles or so from our destination, he might have just enough luck on his side to get them where they're going. But if we arrive in Oregon City and find they've encountered disaster, I won't be at all surprised."

"Especially when you consider some of those with him," Wiser added.

"Luke Suttle is a capable man. And Walter Brown," Elias said.

"Marcus Weiss?" Wiser asked pointedly.

"No, not him," Elias chuckled.

"Well, I don't wish them any harm," Solomon said. "But I don't doubt that the better decision was made by those of us who chose to remain under your care."

13

"Thief!" Marcus Weiss shouted.

Dusk had settled in around the Smith Party's wagons, and the emigrants were busy with their dinners, getting their beds ready for the night. There was a high sense of expectation permeating the camp. They'd reached the road, and while they were prepared for an arduous journey ahead, they were excited that they'd come to the final leg of their long and trying journey.

Jeb Smith paid off Renard, the halfbreed guide they'd hired at The Dalles. The man said he intended to camp there outside the road with them and would return to The Dalles in the morning, though he had urged Smith to hire him as a guide on the road.

"It's a dangerous journey, still. Many river and creek crossings. Dangerous descents and difficult climbs. You would be wise to keep me on until you get to Oregon City," Renard said. "I'll offer you a fair price."

"We can manage it from here," Jeb Smith confidently told him.

Though Renard said he intended to camp with them, Smith noticed later that the man had saddled his horse as if he intended to leave soon. Then he'd lost sight of their guide, but he wasn't worried about Renard. He'd concluded his transaction with the man and had no more need of him. When he left or where he'd gotten to made no difference to Jeb Smith.

Back in The Dalles, Smith had found a wagon to buy for half of what a wagon would have cost him in Missouri. There were plenty of wagons in The Dalles, abandoned by emigrants who didn't want to pay the price to raft their wagon down the river or chose to hurry along the road without the encumbrance of a wagon.

Smith, though, was thinking about the coming winter. He wanted a wagon when they reached Oregon City just in case he would need to house his family in it until he could get a cabin built. He'd also worried that prices in Oregon City might be even higher than those in The Dalles where abandoned wagons and kegs of nails and even stoves and furniture were plentiful, and so he'd bought provisions to last his family through at least part of the winter.

He was in the wagon now, cinching ropes to be sure everything was tied down, when he heard Marcus Weiss shout.

Jeb came out of his wagon with a knife in hand.

His eyes fell immediately on Weiss and Luke Suttle, the two of them wrestling Renard to the ground.

Renard was a small man, anyway. Short with a thin frame. He was wiry, but not powerful enough to overcome Suttle and Weiss together.

Others were rushing into the fray as well, and Jeb made for the commotion.

"What the devil's the problem here?" Jeb shouted.

"I caught him!" Marcus Weiss shouted. "I caught him inside my wagon."

Jeb turned his eyes on Renard. The man's cheek was bleeding where someone had thrown a punch at him, and his clothes were dirty where they'd wrestled him to the ground. Currently, Renard was on the ground on his back, and Luke Suttle kneeled on him with one knee in his stomach and a hand holding Renard's wrist against the ground.

"Tell them to turn me loose!" Renard demanded, squirming to try to get free from Luke Suttle.

"What's happening here?" Jeb Smith asked, looking to Weiss for an answer.

"I caught him snooping around in my wagon," Weiss said. "He had this in his hand!"

Weiss held up a knife, an ornate thing with brass fittings and a leather and brass scabbard.

"He took it from your wagon?" Jeb Smith asked.

"He certainly did. This was my grandfather's knife, brought from Germany."

"I wasn't stealing it," Renard argued.

Walter Brown was coming forward now, leading Renard's horse. The horse was saddled.

"Look at this," Brown said. He reached into one of the saddlebags and came out with a purse with coins in it.

"That's mine!" another of the emigrants called out. "That was in my wagon!"

As they continued going through Renard's saddlebags, they found another purse with coins that another emigrant in the wagon train claimed and also a silver necklace that belonged to one of the women.

"He's a thief!" Marcus Weiss declared again.

"What do you intend to do about it?" Suttle asked, still pinning the man to the ground.

Jeb Smith shook his head and sighed audibly.

"I don't know," he said. "We've taken back the stolen items. I suggest before the man leaves, everyone should make an inventory of their valuables and we should be sure he hasn't taken anything else."

But Marcus Weiss reached into the driver's box of his wagon and came out with a whip in his hand.

"I know what to do with a thief!" he declared. He swung the whip, and Luke Suttle had to fling himself out of the way to avoid being struck.

Weiss lashed the man twice more; Renard throwing up his arms to cover his face and rolling over to offer his back. Weiss swung the whip again, striking the man's back. And again.

"Stop that!" Jeb Smith shouted, but Marcus Weiss was livid and had no intention to stop. He cracked the whip again, this time ripping the man's shirt and drawing blood on from Renard's shoulder.

A couple of men grabbed at Weiss, and Jeb Smith rushed over and wrestled the whip from his hands.

Renard took the opportunity to get to his feet. He pushed at Walter Brown and then sprang for his saddle. No one made any effort to stop him. No one who'd seen the man whipped felt inclined to stop him, especially after his saddlebags had been searched. Renard scrambled to get a foot into a stirrup and his horse was starting to walk away even as he swung himself into the saddle. And then he was riding off in the darkness.

"Stop him!" Marcus Weiss shouted, but no one moved.

ZEKE WAS ABOUT HALF asleep when his horse snorted.

He opened his eyes and felt around on the blanket beside him until his hand touched the leather holster of his Colt Paterson. He slid the revolver from the holster, turned the cylinder one time to take it off the empty chamber, and then he thumbed back the hammer, exposing the trigger. Then he sat up on his blanket and listened to the darkness.

Duke stepped nervously on the ground.

"It's all right," Zeke whispered to the horse. "Don't make any noise. Let me hear."

He'd made up a pretty good campfire with branches he'd collected from brush growing down by the creek in the hollow below. He'd thought the campfire would help to keep him warm through the night. Zeke now wished he'd let the thing burn down. It was just coals now, but glowing coals that would reveal him to anyone riding nearby.

In a moment, Zeke heard another horse not far away snort back at Duke, and his stomach dropped. He didn't know if he was more frightened by a wild animal or a person, but he knew now it was a person out there in the darkness.

"Hello?" a voice called from maybe twenty yards away. "Mind if I ride up?"

"Who is it?" Zeke asked, realizing the absurdity of the question. He was two-thousand miles from most the people he knew. The voice was coming up from the south and his brother and the rest of the wagon train were behind him to the north. There was small chance Zeke would know the person coming toward him.

"It's Renard. Who are you?"

Renard! The halfbreed guide they'd wanted to hire back at The Dalles but had been hired by Jeb Smith ahead of them.

"My name's Townes," Zeke said. "I'm scouting ahead of a wagon train, trying to find the Barlow Road."

"You're not far from it now," Renard said.

In the dim light from the moon and stars, Zeke could see the man now. He was coming on foot, leading his horse.

"You got supper to share?" Renard asked. "I ain't had none and I'm riding without supplies."

"Sure," Zeke said. "Bacon and biscuits. I'd like to see your hand as you walk up."

Renard pinched the horse's reins between his thumb and palm and held both hands high, fingers spread wide, so that Zeke could see his hands were empty.

"I ain't armed," he said.

"I am," Zeke said.

Renard stopped, and Zeke could see him looking for a weapon in Zeke's hands. He held the Colt a little higher where the light hit it.

"You going to rob me?" Renard asked.

"This is just for my own protection," Zeke said.

"You won't need it with me," Renard said. "I'd be glad if you would feed me, and then I'll be on my way."

"You're traveling at night?"

"I'm in a hurry," Renard said.

Zeke let down the hammer on the gun and rotated the cylinder back to the empty chamber. He picked up the holster from his blanket and buckled it around his waist. Then he dropped the Colt down into the holster.

"Let's get you something to eat here," Zeke said. He gathered up some of his firewood and put it down into the fire pit he'd made, on top of the amber coals, and then blew on the coals until the wood started to catch. "I can't offer you much, but I'm happy to share what I've got."

Renard dropped the saddle from his horse's back and then took a seat on the ground near Zeke fire. In the light, Zeke could see the man looked like he'd taken a beating.

"You hurt?"

"I'm all right," Renard said bitterly. "I got into a scuffle over payment from a party I was guiding down to the Barlow Road."

"They refused to pay you?" Zeke asked.

"We had a disagreement over it," Renard said.

Zeke remembered what the blacksmith had said to them when he suggested they find Renard. He'll steal from you, the man had said, referring to Renard. Zeke wondered if Renard had tried to steal from Smith or someone in Smith's wagon train.

He put some bacon and a biscuit in a pan and heated it on the fire.

Renard winced as he ate, clearly his fresh cuts causing him pain. Neither man talked much. Zeke wondered how he would deal with Renard. He didn't care for the idea of a stranger and reputed thief sharing his camp. Even if the man left, as he said he would, Zeke wasn't sure that he'd be able to get any sleep knowing that the man was out here.

"You don't have to worry about me," Renard said, as if he could read Zeke's mind. He talked with his mouth full of biscuit. "I won't stay long. I appreciate the food, but I've got to hurry back to The Dalles."

"What are you in a hurry for?" Zeke asked.

"I've got a job to get to. Never should have agreed to take that wagon train down to the road. But they come with a sob story about arriving late, worried that they'll be stuck in The Dalles until spring. So I took them, even though I knew I shouldn't."

Though he winced through his physical wounds, Zeke could tell that the humiliation of the beating he took at the hands of the emigrants stung far worse than the cuts.

"I'll be on my way now," Renard said with a last bite of bacon.

"Can I give you some food to take with you?"

"I don't need it," Renard said. "I'll be where I'm going by morning."

Zeke watched the man leave and then followed him some distance to be sure he was actually going. Still, Zeke did not do more than doze that night, always on alert and trusting Duke to warn him should Renard decide to turn around and come back. He'd deliberately left Towser and Mustard with the wagons, worried they might expose him to Smith's party and cause some trouble. But he wished now the dogs were with him. They'd let him know if Renard came back.

One thing or the other wasn't true. There was no way, walking or riding, that Renard would be back to The Dalles by morning. If he walked his horse through the night and rode during the day, he could probably be back by mid-afternoon. So either he was wrong about when he would arrive back at The Dalles, or he was lying about his destination. And if he was lying about his destination, Zeke wondered, where else could he be bound for?

14

Five dollars for each wagon and ten cents a head of livestock. It was a small fortune Elias paid at the gatehouse.

A man and his family lived there at the gatehouse, collecting tolls for Barlow. Elias counted at least six children who looked like stair steps, all of them roughly two years apart. But so far as Elias could see, the man had no wife, and Elias began to wonder if the children were his children or if they were hired hands working the place. The man's name was Strickland. The farm suggested he'd been here at least a couple of years, but the farm wasn't yet large enough to do more than support himself and the children.

"It's a good road," Strickland promised. "Of course, it's a new road, and the most important thing to the men building it was speed. So there's some places that'll bounce the teeth right out of your head if you choose to ride in the wagons. Last wagon train through here, a couple of days ago, they said they lost the trail in the Blue Mountains. No fear of getting off the road here, though. From here to Oregon City, the trees are so thick you won't be able to turn left or right off the trail."

"Thick trees is good," Elias said. "My family and I have come west to build a sawmill and cut timber."

"You'll be rich men in no time, the way this territory is growing," the man said. "I come out here twenty years ago as a soldier at Fort Vancouver.

Back then, you could walk a thousand miles without every finding a white man. Now, they're all over, and more and more coming every year."

The man at the gatehouse pulled open the gate, and Henry Blair walked his horse across the bridge over Gate Creek.

"Get those oxes moving," Elias told Gabriel, and the boy gave a call to the oxes and tugged on the yoke of the front ox and snapped his whip and shouted again, and the oxen started to move. The bridge was plenty wide for the wagon to cross, and Elias didn't worry that Gabe could keep the wagon straight the way he might have two thousand miles ago. The hooves sounded heavy on the boards of the bridge.

Strickland stood beside Elias and watched the wagon for a moment.

"Ain't much for forage once you're on the road, but so long as you don't delay too bad it shouldn't be a problem. You just keep them wagons moving, and you'll be all right."

Jason Winter drove his wagon across next, and then Johnny Tucker. Cody Page drove Sophie Bloom's wagon across behind Johnny Tucker. And then came the McKinney brothers in their wagons.

Between each wagon, a handful of people would cross. Most walked, but some went on horseback. The horses, most of them, didn't care much for the bridge, and even Tuckee balked at crossing when Elias first started across.

"It's a rugged road," Strickland called to Elias as he crossed the bridge. "Keep that in mind, and be sure you're scouting the way ahead. There's a good hill called Laurel Hill where you'll have to lower your wagons by rope, and a couple of steep climbs where you'll have to double or triple team the wagons going uphill. But you'll be all right."

Elias threw up a casual wave to the man.

"I appreciate the advice," he called back.

They were starting out two days behind the Smith Party, having camped outside the gatehouse the previous night. It was morning now, but the sun had been up a couple of hours and the Townes Party was getting a later start to the day than they might have.

Gate Creek wasn't much of a body of water, just a little stream, but it did cut a deep and narrow ravine. A wagon wouldn't get across here without the bridge – maybe farther downstream – and it made the perfect place for a gate for the toll road. There wouldn't be any easy way to avoid paying the man.

Once across the bridge, the hilly landscape dominated by empty fields and bunch grass began to change. They were coming now into a thick forest, and by mid-morning the emigrants were surrounded on both sides by pines and spruce and fir reaching high into the sky, virgin growth that had never seen a steel ax blade before Barlow and his crew came through.

"Barlow's attitude was to cut and burn everything in his path," Elias remarked to Gabriel.

The blackened trunks of the trees surrounding the road suggested the fires had gotten away from them several times.

"It's a wonder they didn't burn down every forest in the Cascades," Wiser McKinney said.

Barlow also decided to level out his road through the use of his customers. Rocks and roots and holes jolted anyone brave enough to ride in the wagons. Those walking, if they didn't pay close attention, earned scuffed knees for their carelessness.

"I've avoided fewer dangerous holes coming through prairie dog towns than traveling down this road," Zeke said from Duke's back.

Throughout their time on the Barlow Road, Elias had to abandon his goal of getting close to twenty miles a day. Possible on the prairie, here it was an impossibility. At least a couple of times a day, a tree grew up right in the middle of the road. Wiser McKinney joked that Barlow must have had extra narrow wagons. When they encountered one of these, the wagons would come to a halt, and either they would have to squeeze around the trees, often driving wagon wheels on one side up and over embankments or other obstacles, or as often as not, out came the axes and the Townes Party went to work improving Barlow's road.

No single mile was free of debris or obstacles. Strickland swore there'd been more than a hundred wagons come down the road this year ahead of the Townes Party, but Elias wondered how they'd achieved it. The road wasn't a road. It was an Indian trail that Barlow's road crew had cleaned up some.

They crossed a dry creek bed filled with boulders, and it was almost one of the smoother parts of the road. They came to Deep Creek, which proved to be shallow, but the drop down into the ravine was deep and required the wagons to take the slope at an angle with men working ropes to keep the wagons from toppling over. The animals strained to get the wagons up the far side of the creek. The road was passable, but it wasn't easy.

Still, the emigrants took solace from the fact that they were moving and not stuck back at The Dalles, at someone else's mercy.

Late in the afternoon, Elias turned Tuckee back toward his brother and rode along with Zeke for a while.

"Have you seen the size of some of these trees?" Elias said. "They're a mile tall and straight as they can be."

"We've come to a timberman's paradise," Zeke said.

THE ROAD FOLLOWED ALONG on the north side of the White River, though most of that first day the Townes Party remained far enough from the river that they didn't lay eyes on it or even know it was there. Neither did they lay eyes on Mount Hood. Once they were within the forest, the canopy from the spruce and pine grew so thick that they never had a sighting of the mountain all through the day.

If Elias had envisioned a slow going with many delays as the wagon train navigated steep descents and difficult climbs, he found himself pleasantly surprised when he called for a stop at the end of the first day on the Barlow Road. It had been a mostly straight shot through the woods, following along a ridge that kept pretty level. He guessed they'd only made nine or ten miles. The rough road didn't make for quick travel. And when he did call for a stop, the emigrants found themselves on a ridge and, for the first time, overlooking the White River which flowed down past them from almost due north.

"River must come down off the mountain and then cut east somewhere down below us," Elias said.

"I'd love to climb up on the side of that mountain and get a look at this terrain from up there," Zeke said. "No map makes it hard to imagine what it must look like."

"I'm wondering if this is what our timber plot is going to look like," Elias said.

"If it's even half this well timbered, we've done well, brother."

The emigrants made their camp in a clearing beside the trail that had probably been a camp for Barlow's road crew.

Elias walked among the wagons to check on the families in his charge. He found that spirits were high among the travelers. Everyone had reprovisioned, either at Baxter's mission or at The Dalles. They all had fresh food and felt the excitement of nearing the end of their journey.

The McKinney brothers, who intended to farm in the Willamette Valley, found themselves nervous now in the same way the Townes brothers had been back on the prairie where there wasn't a single tree on the horizon in any direction.

"This isn't farmland," Wiser McKinney said. "The land agent we spoke to back home, he assured us the valley offered the finest farmland on the continent."

Zeke and Marie took their young son and picked their way down the steep hill toward the river below them. It wasn't easy getting down to the river. With Daniel's hand in his, Zeke had to turn his feet against the slope and go down sideways, and in a couple of places he had to move from tree to tree to brace himself. Marie slipped once and landed on her backside, but she only looked up at her husband and laughed.

When they reached the riverbanks, they were both glad they made the effort.

With the river flowing down from the north here, they had their first open view of the day and standing enormous in front of them was Mount Hood.

The peak of Mount Hood stood there, granite and glacier-white against the fading blue sky, and framed by two lower mountains, one left and one right, both painted in the dark green of the spruce and red cedars that covered them. The river ran milky white and foamy with its quick current, split here and there by a rock reaching up from its bottom.

The tall, straight spruce and pines grew all the way down to the river-banks where moss and fern created a soft bed. Hardwoods fought here for the sun's attention but only in places did the hardwoods win out over the evergreens, and in the fall, they colored the riverbanks with orange and yellow and red.

"Oh, my," Marie breathed when she caught Zeke looking toward the north, his head tilted back as if he was watching a bird. She turned and saw Mount Hood, now, towering so far above them. "It's just beautiful Zeke. I cannot believe this is going to be our home."

"It's a blessed life we're living, Marie," Zeke said. "I think of my grandfather – he couldn't imagine the things I've seen these last few weeks. The prairies and the Rocky Mountains. He never dreamed any of this existed in this world."

"It's like we're in the Alps in France," Marie said. "Do you think this river starts on the mountain?"

"It does. We could follow this river right up the side of the mountain to those glaciers we see. It's the glacier that turn it this milky white color in the summer and early fall."

"Who told you that?" Marie laughed at him.

"That man back at the gate. Strickland? He was telling me. He said, too, that if we followed the White River downstream, back into the Tygh Valley, that there's some pretty waterfalls."

"I'm sorry we missed them," Marie said.

"Maybe we'll come back one day," Zeke said. "This place won't be so far from home that we couldn't come back here, maybe camp for a few days."

They'd walked right up to the bank of the river now, and Zeke squatted down onto his knees and stuck a hand in the river.

"Wow! That's cold water," Zeke said.

"How far are we?"

Zeke dried his hand on his pants.

"Seventy miles," Zeke said. "Thereabouts."

Marie laughed.

"After this journey down the Emigrant Trail, I'm not sure I'll ever want to go more than two or three miles from home again. But if I decide I do, I'll let you take me camping to see the White River waterfalls."

Zeke nodded his head.

"I can understand the sentiment," Zeke said. "I bet we can find some waterfalls closer to home once we're settled."

The couple marveled at the sight for quite a while longer, even as dusk began to settle in.

Zeke had found a rock to sit on, and he had Daniel in his lap. The little boy was looking up at Mount Hood, and Zeke was pointing at it and repeating, "Mountain," to him and the boy tried to mimic the word.

Zeke remarked to Marie that he wished Daniel was older and might better remember the trip when something on the far bank caught his attention.

"What is it?" Marie asked, following his line of vision.

"I'm not for sure," Zeke said, squinting his eyes. A few feet inside the trees, and everything became dark shadows, and Zeke couldn't make out anything now. "I'm sure I saw some movement."

"A bear?" Marie asked. Bears, especially here in the mountains, had replaced Natives as everyone's worst fear.

"I don't think so."

Zeke kept his eyes on the far bank. He lifted Daniel up from his lap and set the boy on his own feet. Marie took Daniel by the hand, a worried look across her face.

"What do you think you saw?" Marie asked.

"I think I saw a man moving over there in the woods," Zeke said. "Maybe a couple of men."

"Indians?" Marie asked in the same breathless tone that she asked Zeke if he'd seen a bear.

"Men," Zeke said. "I don't know more than that. It's nothing to worry about. Maybe I didn't see anything. Maybe it's Smith's wagon train camped on the other side of the river."

"But they're two days ahead of us," Marie said.

Zeke shrugged.

"Who knows what twists and turns the road might take?" he said. "Maybe it goes five miles north to find a decent river crossing. It's nothing to worry about. Take one more look at the mountain, and then let's go up and get our supper started. We'll be cooking in the dark at this point."

They climbed back up the slope with the same difficulties they had coming down. Partway up, Zeke had to pick up Daniel and tote him.

"How's the river?" Elias asked.

"Wet and cold, Elias," Zeke said. "It runs pretty fast, and it looks deep enough there. I don't know what the crossing will look like, but I'd be worried about a wagon getting swept away in that current."

Elias frowned.

"That's not a promising report."

"Huh," Zeke said. "I didn't see any wagons floating past, so I'm guessing Smith and his folks made it across. If they can do it, we surely can."

Elias nodded his head.

"It's worth going down there and having a look," Zeke told Elias. "Maybe in the morning, when the sun is up and before we get rolling, you should take your family down and look to the north."

"I'll do it," Elias said.

"One more thing?" Zeke said.

"Sure."

"Double the guard tonight."

HENRY BLAIR RODE FORWARD of the wagon train as they set out the next morning, but he returned even before the back wagons had started to move.

"The trail drops down into the White River valley," Henry told Elias. About a mile ahead, we ford the river."

"How's the ford?" Elias asked him.

"It's just downstream of a big bend in the river, and it's kind of a wide spot, so the river ain't too deep there. We can get the wagons through, but I wouldn't count on making many miles today."

Elias clenched his jaw and shook his head. He glanced at Maddie, on her horse near enough to hear the conversation between the two.

"I suppose our days of making twenty miles a day are behind us," Elias said. "I'm going to have to be prepared to settle for five or ten miles."

"Yes, sir, Mr. Townes," Henry said. "I reckon that's right. We paid to be on a road, but it's hardly better than an old Indian trail."

Elias rode back to Zeke, passing the word along the wagon train as he went that they were approaching a river crossing and the emigrants should be prepared to stop about a mile up the road. Then he and Zeke rode forward with Henry Blair so that they could see the crossing for themselves.

As Henry had said, the crossing came just past a big bend in the river, almost a ninety degree turn, that dramatically slowed the current. The river also opened up wide, making it shallower.

Zeke rode Duke out across the ford, the horse stepping carefully the whole way. He could feel when loose rocks caused Duke to lose his footing.

But they made the other bank, and Duke stepped up the side. Zeke looked around at the landing. The slope wasn't too bad, they would have space to bring the wagons up out of the river. All things considered, it wasn't a bad river crossing, but they would definitely lose time here. Each wagon would have to come across on its own. The bank western bank would churn as the animals and wagons came up out of the river, and by the end of the day it would be a muddy mess. In fact, it was already a mess with wagon wheel ruts and hoof tracks.

Zeke stepped Duke back across the river. The water never came up higher than the horse's knees.

"Nothing to do but to cross it," Zeke reported. "There's some loose rocks in the riverbed, but nothing out of the ordinary. No big boulders to avoid or anything like that."

"Good," Elias said. "It looks like a good crossing."

The only catch in the crossing was that just before they entered the river, the wagons had to make a sharp turn. The road some distance back took them down into the river valley where they drove parallel to the river for a ways, and here at the crossing, the eastern wall of the river valley rose up sharply, something close to two hundred feet. There wasn't room to make an easy, gradual turn, and wagons didn't do well with sharp turns. That turn forced every wagon to come to a complete stop before making the crossing.

"We'll be here all day," Elias muttered as he watched Gabriel maneuver the turn and drive the oxen into the river.

The stop did allow for those walking to climb aboard their wagons. The water was so cold that no one wanted to walk it.

Once the wagons made the far side, Zeke sent them forward down the road where it continued alongside the White River, but now west of the river. The slope here to the ridge above wasn't nearly as severe as the slope on the east side, and the road snaked along a ridge midway up the slope.

They were traveling almost straight north, now, though the only evidence most of the emigrants had of their direction of travel came from the glimpses they got of Mount Hood directly in front of them. And as they made it farther along the road, and the canopy of the trees overhead grew thicker, those glimpses of the mountaintop became more rare.

Gradually, the road climbed to the top of the western ridge. As it did, the river valley grew more narrow. The river got rougher, tumbling and crashing over rocks and around twists. The logic in the location of the crossing became plenty obvious. Barlow had crossed in one of the few places where he could.

They camped about six miles from where they'd started the day.

15

SOPHIE BLOOM STEPPED CAUTIOUSLY through fallen branches and thick pine straw as she walked with her children toward the river. She was becoming uncomfortable now as her pregnancy progressed. So far, other than the sickness in the first few weeks, the pregnancy had not been a terrible deterrent to the travel. But now her back ached. Now her stomach protruded enough that she felt weighed down. She'd caught herself riding in the wagon more, especially in those days from the Blue Mountains to the mission and then to The Dalles. But on this rough road, all that bouncing around, she worried that the constant jarring might be dangerous for the unborn baby, and so she walked.

The camp that afternoon sat between the road and the river in a fairly level piece of ground that had obviously been used as a camp by Barlow and his crew and probably every other wagon train that had come through this way so far. It was an ideal spot for a camp with easy access to the river for watering livestock and washing. It also provided a nice view of Mount Hood up above them, closer now but less of it showing with the high hill between the camp at the glacial mountain peak.

"The High Cascades," Cody Paige said, coming down from the camp to join Sophie and her children.

"What's that?" Sophie said, turning and seeing him there and smiling at him.

"Mount Hood is one of several giant mountains in this range," Cody said. "Mr. Townes was telling me about it. This mountain range is known as the Cascade Mountains, and these giants, like Mount Hood, they're called the 'High Cascades.'"

Sophie wrinkled her nose as she smiled.

"That's a really pretty name," she said. "The High Cascades."

"Some of them are bigger than Mount Hood," Cody said. "And they say if you climb high enough up the side of it, you can see some of the others even though they're a hundred miles away."

"I cannot imagine," Sophie said.

"Can't imagine what?"

"A bigger mountain. Nor can I imagine climbing up the side of it."

"How are you doing?" Cody said with a glance at Sophie's stomach.

"Oh, I'm miserable, Mr. Page. Truly. Everything aches. I did not know I was pregnant when we set out across the Missouri River in late April. By the time I did realize, we were still hoping to reach Oregon City by September. I thought it would be unpleasant but not impossible to make the journey in my condition. Now, of course, I'm wishing I had gone back."

Cody's face must have dropped a touch.

"Oh, I don't mean that," Sophie quickly said. "It's been such a pleasure to get to know you, Mr. Page, and share this journey with you. I'm so grateful to you. I only mean that my feet hurt and my back aches so terribly."

Cody nodded his head.

"Yes, ma'am," he said. "I reckon so. I'm sorry for you that we've been so delayed these last few weeks."

"But we're almost there, now," Sophie said. "Almost to the end of our journey."

"I'm ready for it," Cody said.

"I can't believe you will be working in this forest," Sophie said, looking around at the trees. "I've never seen so many trees, and so tall."

"It'll be an experience," Cody said. "I'm ready to get started. This has been too much time tending to animals for me. If I'd wanted to tend to animals like this, I'd have been a ranch hand instead of a timberman."

"I wonder how far your logging camp will be from my sister's farm," Sophie said.

"I don't know, Miss Sophie. But it don't matter how far it is."

"Why is that, Mr. Page?"

"I intend to come and see you as often as I can," Cody said. "If you'll have me."

"Of course, I will."

At that moment, both Cody and Sophie jumped at the bark of a rifle shot. The sound came from downstream, but not far away. Cody turned around, craning his neck to see. Sophie reached out and grabbed his arm with both hands, clinging to him.

"Is it Savages?" she asked.

"More likely a bear," Cody said.

Then another gunshot, and this one followed by some whoops and laughter. Cody still couldn't see beyond a bend in the river and the trees, but he reached out his other hand and touched Sophie's fingers on his arm.

"I think it's okay," he said. "I'm just going to walk down a ways and see what's happening."

He picked his way through the trees near the bank until he could see a half dozen or so men from the wagon train standing on the riverbank.

One of them was pulling a large fish from a net, and another was pointing a rifle into the river. Even as he watched, the hammer fell on the rifle. A cloud of white smoke and another thunder of the rifle. Several of the men laughed and clapped, and the man with the net shoved it quickly into the river, bringing out another fish.

"What is that?" Cody called to them. It was Wiser McKinney who called back to him.

"We're fishing for trout!"

Cody hurried back to set Sophie Bloom's mind at ease.

"Neither bear nor Indians," he said. "They're shooting trout out of the river."

THE EMIGRANTS ENJOYED A great feast that evening.

They'd shot a dozen trout out of the river and more than that they'd pulled out on fishing lines. A couple of intrepid men managed to reach into the river and grab a trout, though they'd lost as many with that technique as they'd managed to capture. Wood was so plentiful that they cooked the fish over a community fire rather than each family making their own, and then when supper was finished, they built the fire up again.

They all declared the fish to be the best they'd ever had, though they'd said the same about the salmon back on the Snake River.

The McKinney brothers played their guitars, and Jeff Pilcher reluctantly tapped a keg of whiskey he'd bought in The Dalles and intended for himself once he was settled in his new home. The other emigrants gave him no sympathy and drank liberally of his liquor, and a few others who had their own stock passed around bottles.

Madeline, who had a fine singing voice, entertained with the McKinney brothers backing her.

Marie and some of the other women started a dance, and a few of the men who'd had a share of Pilcher's whiskey gave their wives a turn or two on the makeshift dance floor.

Someone urged Elias Townes to make a speech and soon many others took up the chant.

"Friends," he started, standing near the fire where all could see him. "I think back tonight to mid-April, when my brother and I and our small party of family and friends arrived in St. Joseph. Not a wagon captain to be found who was fit to hire. I thought then that months and months of planning and preparing and dreaming had been spent in waste. And there I met several of you for the first time, Wiser and Solomon, Jefferson, and some of you others – and some others who are a day or two ahead of us – and you convinced me that we were all an enterprising lot and we could make the journey without an experienced captain. And we came upon young Mr. Henry Blair who agreed to act as our guide. You gave me the distinct honor of leading this wagon train, and I'd like to think that in the many weeks from then to now, we've gone from strangers to friends to family. It never was my ambition to captain a wagon train, and I don't know what others who have taken on the duty would have to say about it, but for my part, I can testify that each of you made it the easiest of jobs to undertake. You pitched in and did your part, you kept your grumbling to a low roar, and I've thoroughly enjoyed your company. As I said, I consider you all my family, and I hope whatever futures await us in Oregon that in the years ahead our fellowship will continue. That in times of sorrow or joy, you'll feel free to come to me and to each other with heavy hearts or with celebrations. We've made this journey together, and we'll forever be bonded by these days. I'm grateful to all of you."

The speech drew applause and handshakes, and promises of forever continuing familial relations. Wiser McKinney grabbed Henry Blair by the arm and took him over near the fire.

"Let me just say, what a fantastic job this young man has done," Wiser said, clapping Henry on the shoulder. "We've all called on him at one time or another to help us out, and he's been an incredible servant to this wagon train. Hip! Hip!"

The crowd cheered for Henry, and turned their handshakes on him.

Others, too, made speeches. Jefferson Pilcher recalled their attention to the South Pass incident where Pilcher and a couple of other families had fallen behind thanks to a broken axle. They were set upon by scalp hunters and vengeful Indians full of rage, and it was Zeke Townes who saved them all. Another round of cheers went up for Zeke.

Zeke thanked the men in the cow column who had dutifully kept and cared for the livestock.

Someone said a word for those they'd lost to accident or murder, and the mood became a bit more somber. People patted Stephen Barnes – whose daughter was murdered at Soda Springs – and hugged Sophie Bloom whose husband had met with an accident a few days out from Bridger's Fort.

Captain Walker enlivened the mood again by speaking of the future.

"We've all come to this new territory for our own reasons. Some plan to become merchants while others intend to till the soil. The Townes brothers plan to earn their living felling trees, and we can plainly see they've got their work cut out for them. Whatever lays ahead of you, I'd like to offer my best wishes and echo what Mr. Townes had to say. It's been a unique pleasure to journey so far with you good people, and I hope our acquaintance lasts to the end of our days."

At some point in the evening, when Elias and Zeke were sitting together with their families, Elias leaned over and patted Zeke on the knee.

"I suppose I owe Jeb Smith a debt of gratitude," Elias said, not so loud as to be overheard by anyone.

"Is that right?" Zeke asked him with a grin. "And why is that?"

"Because of him, I get to finish this overland journey with the families I enjoy spending time with. I don't miss any of those others, nor the problems they brought. Have you noticed how pleasant the last couple of days have been? Since we left The Dalles, honestly. No complaints. No back-biting or gossiping. Everyone is just doing his part to get us to Oregon City. It's been exceedingly delightful."

With fresh provisions and now within a hundred miles or so of their destination, the Townes Party enjoyed a joyous afternoon and evening like they'd not had in some weeks. For many of them, this would be the day they recalled in later years as the best of the entire journey.

The next day, everything changed.

16

Solomon McKinney in a hushed voice spoke to Elias.

"I think we must have clouds blowing in," he said. "When I started the watch, I could still see stars, and now there's none."

"Could be," Elias said, looking up for the stars and finding only darkness there.

The two men shared the second watch of the night up near the front of the wagons. Jeff Pilcher and Caleb Driscoll had the watch on the other end of the wagons, and some of the men working the livestock were awake with the animals.

Elias had hoped they wouldn't see rain again until they were safely down in the Willamette Valley. He didn't know what the Barlow Road might hold in store for them, but he imagined the hills would likely get steeper. Strickland, the man back at the gatehouse, had said something about Laurel Hill and how it was a tough descent. Elias had hoped the weather would hold, that the worst of what they'd see was back in the Blue Mountains.

"If it's rain coming, it'll be cold," Solomon said. "And maybe snow, as high up as we are."

"All the more reason to keep these wagons moving," Elias said. "Strickland, the man at the tollhouse? He told me that Barlow tried this time last year to take this route to Oregon City. There was no road, at that time. Barlow didn't construct the road until this spring. They were cutting their way through as they went. Strickland said they sent a party up the slopes of the mountain to try to scout the way ahead. Finding no good route, they returned to their camp and all but two of them returned to The Dalles. Those two stayed with their supplies for the winter."

"Did they?" Solomon said, surprised. "Did they survive it?"

"They did," Elias said. "They built a cabin for the two men and returned in the spring to collect their things and build this road."

"We could probably last through the winter," Solomon said. "If we had to. But I'd rather not put it to the test."

"Nor would I," Elias said. "We just have to keep moving and it won't be a problem."

Another hour, and Elias woke Wiser and Captain Walker to take the next shift.

He didn't have any trouble falling to sleep. But when he woke the next morning, he could hear the pitter patter of rain drops hitting the canvas tent.

Before sunup, Wiser McKinney started making noise outside to roust out the emigrants. Wiser was always good about waking the others when he had last watch. He'd collect some firewood and drop it on the ground. Then he'd mumble to himself as he started trying to get the fire lit. Then he'd speak loudly to whoever had watch with him. Then he'd get a kettle to make coffee and he'd bang it on a rock or against the side of a wagon a couple of times. Gradually building the noise until people were waking up. It was a kindness to the women, Wiser confided to Elias all the way back when they were following the Platte River.

"If we were just a party of men, I'd bang the pots and shout at the morning light and have everyone up and awake immediately. But with women here, I like to be kind about it, wake them slowly so that those who want can laze in their beds for a little while."

He'd reached the stage of calling across the camp to Captain Walker when Elias blinked at the darkness inside the tent.

"Do you have coffee beans enough, Captain?" Elias heard Wiser shout.

"Fine, sir. Plenty of coffee. Almost time for reveille."

"Almost," Wiser called back.

Elias fumbled in the dark some, trying not to make noise. He struck a match and lit a candle inside a brass lantern. He closed the door on the lantern and looked across the tent at Madeline. She smiled at him as she blinked at the light, and Elias smiled back.

"Is that rain I hear?" Madeline asked.

"It is," Elias said

"It's going to be a cold morning."

"Good morning to ride in the wagon," Elias said.

"Not on this road," Maddie said.

"That may be true. We should get up and get moving."

Elias had noted over the last two thousand miles that the emigrants moved slower in the rain, and now he saw that a cold rain made it even worse.

They were slow to emerge from their tents. They were slow to get their breakfast fires started. The women were slow to cook. The men were slow to get the tents down. They helped each other, though, working together to shake the rainwater from their canvas tents and fold them. They did the best they could to shake the water off, but all of the tents would get stowed still plenty damp. If this rain lasted a few days the tents would start to get musty and moldy.

Elias said a silent prayer for a short-lived rain and sunshine by afternoon.

The men were slow to eat their breakfasts and slow to get their oxen teams hitched.

The first light of day appeared gray all around them. Then the sun's rays struck out into the sky, the sun hidden far below on the eastern horizon.

"It's going to be a long day," Elias warned them. "The sooner we get back on the road, the better. The best way to stay warm is to keep moving."

Elias shivered and hugged himself. When the light of day finally surrounded them, the Townes Party still had not started to move. The clouds above were dark and covered the entirety of the visible sky. Elias felt very cold and very wet.

Elias wondered if Jeb Smith's party had reached Laurel Hill yet. If they'd not yet made the descent, they would surely leave it a muddy mess for Elias and his wagons. Hopefully, he thought, they were down the hill already and it wouldn't be churned to a soup by the time Elias first laid eyes on it.

17

WALTER BROWN KEPT WATCH by himself.

The Smith Party started out from the Baxter Mission keeping regular watches. At least four men working in three hour shifts through the night. Protecting the wagon train from bears and other wild animals. Guarding the livestock to be sure they didn't stampede or wander. But the wagon train didn't have much in the way of livestock – a few horses, a few steers or milk cows, spare oxen, and some sheep. When the wagon train split, most of the livestock belonged to the members of the Townes Party and remained with them.

With a wagon train greatly reduced in numbers, the night watch put a new burden on all the men. Every couple of nights they were losing sleep to their turn on watch. With growing complaints, Jeb Smith decided that three or four men on each watch was unnecessary. With a couple of men keeping watch over the livestock, Jeb Smith decided one man keeping watch at the wagons would be sufficient, and he broke the watch up into two shifts rather than three.

The burden would be greater on those men who lost almost an entire night's sleep, but it would come around less often.

As the clouds rolled in that night, Walter Brown was the lone man to see them.

Wrapped in a blanket against the cold and with his back propped against a wagon wheel through most of his watch, he struggled to stay awake.

He'd become less serious about nighttime noises after shooting his boots with a shotgun back near the Bear River, believing he'd heard a rattlesnake rummaging near them. He'd taken a good amount of ribbing from the others over that, but worse he'd ruined his boots. His feet had been blistered and bloody from walking on boots riddled with holes, and he'd vowed to himself never again to be so easily startled by noises in the dark.

When the rain started, Brown pulled the blanket up over his head like a hooded cloak and nestled in and prayed that morning would come soon.

The minutes ticked interminably. Brown dozed some. The rain woke him. He pulled his blanket tighter around him. The cold woke him. He got up and walked around, keeping the blanket pulled around himself. He returned to his perch at the wagon wheel and started the process over again.

When morning at last broke and the other folks started to rise from their beds, Brown told them it had been raining for at least a couple of hours. He had nothing else to report from the night. Some of the travelers were still in their tents, struggling to rise. Others were just starting their morning routines. All seemed as usual, but with the inconvenience of the cold and rain, until Luke Suttle came searching for Walter Brown.

"Have you seen Angela?" he asked.

"Your nephew's wife?" Brown said. "I haven't seen her."

"She wasn't in the tent when we woke," Suttle said.

Luke Suttle traveled with his nephew Jacob and Jacob's new bride Angela. The couple had been married only a few months when they began their journey west. Luke, never married and with no children of his own, had announced at his brother's home his intention to go west. Jacob quickly latched onto the idea, and the pair spent a year in planning and preparation, a year which included the hurried wedding after Angela refused to be left behind.

"Jacob's beside himself," Luke Suttle said. "He's searching the woods. Did you hear anything overnight?"

"Nothing," Walter said, now feeling a twinge of guilt over those moments when he'd snapped back awake without knowing for how long he had dozed. "I'll go and get Jeb."

As Walter hurried toward Jeb Smith's tent, he heard Jacob Suttle in the woods calling for Angela.

It took only moments before the entire body of the wagon train was searching for the missing girl. Calling her name. Looking in the woods beside the camp. Walking along the Barlow Road in the vicinity of the camp.

Jeb Smith went to the men who'd kept watch over the livestock, but none of them had seen or heard anything in the night.

It wasn't uncommon for people to get up from their tents at night and go into the woods to relieve themselves. Walter Brown could remember a couple of times someone stirring and walking away from their tent into the woods. But he'd paid no mind to them. Why would he?

Jacob Suttle became inconsolably distraught, sobbing as he rushed through the woods shouting his wife's name until at last Luke and some of the others were able to get him under control, convincing him that an orderly search should be made.

18

As the Townes Party began to roll out, leaving the White River and crossing a creek, they saw a cabin in a clearing not far from the road.

Solomon McKinney greeted the sighting of the cabin with great enthusiasm.

"Surely, that's where the two men from the Barlow Party wintered last year with the supplies," McKinney declared.

Together with his brother and their children, Solomon left the wagon train, allowing it to continue on ahead, to explore the cabin. They spent only a few moments looking around the site before rejoining their wives, left in charge of driving their teams.

"The cabin has withstood the summer admirably," Solomon said. "If we needed, we could survive another winter in it."

But the arduous road soon sapped Solomon's enthusiasm.

They had to ford the small creek several times within just a couple of miles. Each crossing caused another few moments of delay for each wagon that had to go across. The crossings were muddy and tedious, and with the rain still falling, at least one wagon got mired at each crossing. And then the delay grew from a few moments to several minutes. Every man in the wagon train walked with mud caked on his boots and sopping pant legs.

"Would it have broken the man's budget for Barlow to build a bridge or two?" Elias muttered to Gabriel.

The boy, though, didn't know enough to complain. The Barlow Road for him was just one more piece of a grand adventure, and Gabe only regretted that it was nearing an end.

The only mercy was that the road followed the creek so the travelers stayed down in the bottoms with the high ridges over them. Had they been required to climb slopes, the day would have been doubly difficult.

Elias guessed they only made something between four and five miles when the road left the creek and took a decidedly unpleasant upward trajectory.

The oxen heaved to pull the wagons, and on the heavier wagons, two beasts had to be added to the teams. Another lengthy delay in the middle of a miserable day.

First, they climbed directly up the slope and then took a turn to take the remainder of the hill to the summit at an angle.

As they climbed the slope, Elias sent Henry Blair ahead to scout the road. Henry returned sooner than Elias had hoped with more bad news.

"The summit is just up yonder," Henry said, twisting in his saddle to point around over his shoulder. "And then the trail drops down the other side. Steeper going down than this is going up."

Elias sighed.

"We'll camp at the summit?" he asked.

"That would be my advice. I don't know how far down we travel, but it'll be a chore, surely."

Elias shook his head.

"I don't think we've come six miles today," he said.

He could envision the difficulties the Barlow Party had experienced a year ago. They'd not made it farther than the cabin. They'd climbed this same slope, and then higher, to the glacial side of Mount Hood where they must have looked down at the hills and valleys, the creeks and gorges, with abject consternation wondering how they could possibly go any farther through this wilderness. Even with a road cut in front of him, Elias felt much the same way right now.

"Think we're ever going to get to Oregon City?" Henry Blair laughed, the rain pattering off the brim of his hat.

"I don't care to talk about it, Henry," Elias said. "Right now, I just want to get to the top of this hill."

When at last they reached the summit, Elias figured they'd climbed no less than eight hundred feet from the point where they left the creek, maybe even a thousand feet. However high, he knew it had been exhausting for all of them – from the children to the oxes, the horses and the men and women. Even Zeke's dogs had no energy for running around as Elias called a halt for the day.

No one rushed to collect firewood or pitch a tent, even though the rain continued to splash on their heads. Instead, everyone in the party took several minutes to catch their breath.

19

Luisa Weiss found Angela Suttle.

The men searching for her had focused their search to the north of their campsite, believing Angela Suttle must have gone in the dark back toward a nearby creek. No one could offer any sort of explanation of why they thought so, but it was where they searched.

Seeking privacy, Luisa Weiss went west of the camp, following the road a little ways, looking for a convenient and secluded place. That's when she saw Luisa Weiss hanging on the trunk of a sturdy pine.

Her shriek brought forth a great commotion of running men and a few of the women from the camp.

Jeb Smith reached her first.

She was still screaming, rooted to the spot in the same way that the pine tree did not sway. Her eyes wide in terror, her screams pausing only for breath. Jeb Smith followed her gaze and saw Angela Suttle's body.

The woman was tied at the neck and waist so tight to the tree trunk that blood stained the ropes. Her clothes hung loosely from her body, ripped and torn. No part of her body escaped the deep cuts that had been made into her flesh – arms and legs, face and torso, were all caked in dark and dried blood. Her eyes had been dug from their sockets, her tongue cut from her gaping mouth.

There could be no doubt that the injuries came at the hand of a man, but none who saw the body would argue that the poor woman was murdered by animals.

By the time Marcus Weiss reached his screaming wife, several of the men who'd run in front of him were already there, staring at the tortured body suspended on the tree trunk.

Weiss merely glanced at the horror on the pine tree before grabbing Luisa by the arm, jerking her around and then slapping her violently across the face so that she fell to the ground. Beth Gordon, who had not seen the body on the tree – but had guessed at what must be there – quickly knelt and collected Luisa from the ground, dragging her to her feet, wrapping an arm around Luisa's head and pushing the woman's face into her shoulder.

"Come here, Mrs. Weiss," Beth Gordon said. "It's going to be all right. Come here and don't look at it."

Luke Suttle saw his nephew's wife hanging there and then hurried to stop Jacob from seeing it for himself. But Jacob would not be stopped, pushing forward to see for himself.

Several of the men could not stomach what they'd seen and dashed away to vomit.

Jacob came to where he could see, and immediately began to sob uncontrollably. Luke took his nephew in his arms and pulled him back, the same as Mrs. Gordon had done with Luisa Weiss.

"We should cut her down," John Gordon said to Jeb Smith, neither man able to take their eyes off the terrible thing in front of them.

"We should," John Gordon said. But neither of the men moved.

Finally, it was Marcus Weiss who took an ax and, walking to the back of the tree, cut the ropes in two chops, allowing the body to drop unceremoniously to the ground.

Jeb Smith gasped blaspheme at the sight of it.

"We should have lowered her to the ground," he muttered to Walter Brown.

Someone turned up with a shovel, and the men took turns digging through the rocky soil and roots. They did not get very deep into the soil.

Hezekiah Smith cut two pieces of board from the side of his wagon and carved Angela Suttle's name into one of the boards and then fashioned a cross from the two boards. Walter Brown's wife brought a blanket to wrap the body in.

Several of the women joined Beth Gordon in trying to console Luisa Weiss. The shock of what she'd seen overwhelmed her. Even back at the wagons, Luisa sat and cried into her hands.

Likewise, Jacob Suttle was beyond control.

He shouted and threw his arms around.

"Savages!" he blamed. And then his eyes fell on the Cayuse they'd hired back at the Baxter Mission. Jacob drew his knife and had to be held back by the others.

"We don't know who did this," Luke Suttle said, holding his nephew back. "Do not compound tragedy with tragedy!"

The entire camp was in chaos.

John Gordon, who was enraged by all he'd seen, armed himself with a rifle and began walking the road ahead in search of the persons responsible. Jeb Smith's sons, both of them nearly adults, also took up rifles and joined Gordon. They were gone and out of sight before Jeb Smith even knew they'd left.

Walter Brown began an investigation, searching for tracks around Jacob's tent. He soon found a footprint that he took to be Angela Suttle's because it was smaller. It was a footprint in the mud, and Brown reasoned that she must have left the tent in the dark to relieve herself.

"The men responsible for this heinous act must have grabbed her when she was away from the camp," Walter Brown decided and said to anyone who would listen to him.

Jacob Suttle at last calmed down and put away his knife. Luke stayed near him, along with Marcus Weiss and Jeb Smith's wife.

And when Smith came to see if Jacob wanted to see his wife before they buried her, the Jacob broke down in sobs again.

Jeb Smith and a couple of the others began piling rocks on top of the body after placing the woman's body in the shallow grave. They used large rocks and piled them much higher than was necessary. Hezekiah used a shovel to hammer his cross into the ground.

By the time things started to settle down some, it was already noon.

Sometime during the morning, the Cayuse retreated without a word, abandoning the wagon train.

"DOES ANYONE KNOW WHERE my husband has gone?" Beth Gordon began asking. She'd fixed her attention on Luisa Weiss and had not seen her husband leave the camp.

"He went in search of the perpetrator," Marcus Weiss said, drawing unexpected attention to himself.

"He did what?" Hezekiah Smith asked. "What kind of foolhardy nonsense is that?"

"He took his rifle and marched up the road," Weiss said.

"That a damn fool thing to do," Hezekiah said with no regard for the worry flashing across Beth Gordon's face. "Go off on his own like that. He'll get hisself killed."

"He wasn't on his own," Weiss said. "Your grandsons went with him."

Hezekiah took this news hurriedly to Jeb Smith who was at that moment still engaged in piling rocks on the dead woman's grave.

"The boys have gone off looking for the murderers," Hezekiah said.

"What boys?" Jeb demanded, a rock the size of his head in his hands.

"Your sons! They went off with John Gordon."

Jeb Smith put the rock down on the grave, shaking his head. The rain was still coming down, though Smith thought it was lighter now than it had been.

"When did they do this?" Smith asked his father.

"I couldn't say, Jeb. Marcus Weiss saw them all going."

"Where did they go?"

"Up the road," Hezekiah said, motioning toward the bend in the road where it turned back to the north to follow a ridgeline.

Jeb Smith closed his eyes, trying to shut out everything long enough that he could think.

"What made them think the people who done this went that away?" he asked. Hezekiah only shook his head helplessly and shrugged his shoulders. "Well, we need to get after them before our problems compound. Were they on foot?"

"I reckon, but you should ask Weiss."

Marcus Weiss offered what little information he could. He'd seen the three of them walking off about half an hour before. Maybe three-quarters of an hour. They'd been on foot, armed with rifles, and he'd heard John Gordon say something about getting justice.

"And you didn't try to stop him?" Jeb Smith asked angrily.

"Warn't my place to stop them," Marcus Weiss said. "So much else going on, I figured you knew what they were doing."

"Well, I didn't," Smith bit back.

Hugh Anderson and Jack Horne were still covering the woman's grave. The rocks were nearly two feet thick over the grave now, and they just kept piling them on with nothing else to do. Both men, like the others, had seen the mutilated body. Neither of them was over twenty-years-old, and the gruesome murder had left them rattled.

"Hugh and Jack, go and fetch us some horses," Jeb Smith said to them. "Better bring me about eight of them."

Smith called for five volunteers to ride with him to go after John Gordon and his own sons.

Walter Brown volunteered immediately. Marcus Weiss agreed when no one else stepped forward. Jacob Suttle also said he would go, and his uncle volunteered right behind him. Jeb Smith objected, said Jacob should stay and Luke should probably stay with him.

"If there's any chance they find the men who did this to my wife, I'm going to be there," Jacob Suttle said.

"You need to rest," Smith said to Jacob. "You've had a terrible shock, son. Rest and take it easy right now, and let us go and do this."

"I'm going with you," Jacob said.

Smith looked to Luke Suttle, silently pleading for help, but Luke just shook his head. He didn't know any better than the rest of them what to say Jacob or what to do. It was a feeling that pervaded the entire camp. No one knew quite what to do.

Those who were going to bring back Smith's sons and John Gordon went to their wagons to fetch rifles, shot, and powder and their saddles.

And when they'd gathered again, Anderson and Horne were just bringing up the horses.

"We've got another problem, Mr. Smith," Hugh Anderson told him.

"What's that?"

"Them Cayuse you hired, I think they've run off."

Jeb Smith dropped his shoulders, feeling completely defeated.

JEB SMITH AND THE others caught up with John Gordon and Smith's two sons about three miles down the road.

"What were you thinking?" Smith asked, ignoring Gordon and speaking to his sons.

Johnny, his oldest and the one he'd named for himself, answered him.

"Mr. Gordon figured based on where the found Mrs. Suttle's body that the attackers must have gone ahead on the road so as not to pass by the camp. We thought maybe we could catch them, or find their trail."

"Did you find anything?" Jacob Suttle demanded, his eyes wild so that he looked half crazed.

"No, sir. We didn't find nothing."

"We've brought you horses," Smith said, nodding to the three saddled horses without riders. "Mount up and let's get back. We've got more problems than a few back at camp."

"What's happened?" John Gordon asked.

Smith, so angry he couldn't speak to Gordon, ignored the man.

"Them Cayuse we hired to drive the livestock have run off," Walter Brown said. "I think they were afraid Jacob was going to accuse them of the murder."

"How do we know they didn't do it?" Jacob said. "Them running off, seems to me they likely did. It's them we should be chasing after right now."

"It wasn't them Cayuse," Luke Suttle said.

"How do you know?" Jacob demanded of his uncle. "Were you watching them? Did you see what they did or didn't do?"

"Whoever did that to poor Angela, they was a mess this morning, covered in blood," Luke said. "I hate to say it to you like that, Jake, but it's the truth. It wasn't them Cayuse."

"These forests are full of Savages," Jeb Smith said. "Surely, your poor wife was the victim of some band of local Indians. All we can do now is pray for her soul and keep moving on to Oregon City."

"We should have some sort of funeral ceremony when we go back," Walter Brown suggested. "We've buried that poor girl without anyone saying a prayer for her."

The two Smith boys mounted their horses, and John Gordon took the reins of the third riderless horse.

"We should find them that done it, and we should punish them for it," John Gordon said with a deliberate look at Jacob Suttle.

"I agree with Mr. Gordon," Jacob said. "I cannot leave these hills with my wife's murder unaccounted for."

"We'll report it in Oregon City," Smith said. "The authorities there will better know how to handle this than we do. They'll have relations with the local Indians, and perhaps they can have the perpetrators handed over to stand trial."

"Won't be no need for a trial if we do what's right ourselves," John Gordon said.

Jeb Smith was about to make an argument. The women and children needed to be gotten to Oregon City before the winter came. The rain should be a warning to them that they must keep moving. If they wanted, Gordon and Jacob Suttle, they could come back to the mountains with a posse from Oregon City, but the women and children needed to move on to civilization. Especially now, he was going to say. He was prepared to make these arguments, and started to, when a distant thump caught their ears.

"Was that gunfire?" Walter Brown said.

"It sounded like gunfire to me," Marcus Weiss said.

Another thump confirmed to them that there was shooting, and that it was coming from the direction of the camp.

"We've got to get back," Walter Brown said, and he wheeled his horse even as John Gordon dashed past him on his horse.

20

"WE SHOULD HAVE STAYED with Elias Townes," Hugh Anderson said.

Jack Horne, chewing on a piece of jerky, chuckled.

"You ain't kidding, partner. You know what's about to happen? You and me are about to be responsible for all these damn horses and oxen and cattle. Every animal in this camp is going to be our duty to deal with until we get to Oregon City."

"Hell, at this point I'm worried about whether we'll even make it Oregon City," Anderson said.

"You ain't worried about Indian attack, are you?" Horne laughed.

"Something killed that woman. You saw her as good as I did. That was vicious."

"It was probably that man Weiss," Horne said. "The way he lays into his wife with his belt. Man has a cruel streak."

"This wasn't no cruel streak," Anderson breathed, his imagination conjuring the sight of Angela Suttle's body hanging from that tree trunk.

"What do you think they did with her tongue and her eyeballs?" Horne asked.

"Hush," Hugh Anderson said, standing up and peering into the woods.

Horne chuckled.

"What's the matter, Hugh? You squeamish over eyeballs and a tongue? I bet them dirty Savages ate 'em."

But Hugh Anderson wasn't paying any attention to him.

"I seen something in the woods."

Horne's natural reaction was to make a quip, but he stopped short seeing the look on Anderson's face. He'd turned pale.

"What is it? A bear?"

Anderson shook his head and turned away now. He walked over to where he had his saddle propped against the trunk of a big pine, and he drew his rifle from a leather scabbard.

"Something's out there," Anderson said.

Horne stood up now, too, peering into the woods. And then he let out a shout as a man came dashing from the shadows of the trees, a rock hammer in his hand. Horne threw up his arms to defend himself and felt the bone splintering blow from the hammer. Horne fell away, twisting as a blinding pain shot up his arm and through his shoulder. He never even got a clear look at the man who wielded the hammer against him. The man raised the hammer high and dropped it with a crushing blow on the back of Horne's skull.

Hugh Anderson loaded the rifle as fast as he could, backing up as he loaded the rifle.

He saw Horne get smashed in the head and realized the attack was not isolated. Down at the camp there were shrieks coming from the women. Some screamed in terror. Others called for their children.

The man who attacked Horne was an Indian, dressed in skins, with ornaments piercing his ears. His long hair was braided on each side of his head and decorated with a single feather in the back. He had a wild look in his eyes.

He stood for a moment over Horne's lifeless body and then gave the hammer another swing, bashing Horne in the skull a second time.

Anderson had retreated back into the woods, watching Horne's murder. With the rifle loaded, Anderson dropped to a knee, drew back the hammer, and raised the rifle to his shoulder. He waited, not even breathing. There were trees in the way, and Anderson didn't have a clear shot. When the Indian turned for him, Anderson would let him come and take the shot when he was sure of it.

But the Indian must not have seen where Anderson went. He looked around for just a moment, and then he started toward the camp. Anderson darted to his feet and rushed forward. The moment he was clear of the trees, he put the rifle to his shoulder again, aimed at the man's back, and squeezed the trigger. The hammer dropped and the cap burst. Then the big rifle spit sparks and a cloud of white smoke.

The heavy bullet smashed into the Indian's back, sending the man sprawling to the ground. He tried to raise himself, but Anderson rushed forward. Using the butt of his rifle, he smashed the man's skull just as he'd done to Jack Horne.

Ahead, at the camp, women and children were running in every direction. Some were being chased, and Anderson saw straight away that this was no Indian attack. At least, it wasn't strictly an Indian attack. Two or three of the attackers in the camp were white men. And then Anderson's eyes fell on a small man, an Indian dressed in regular clothes. And Hugh Anderson recognized the man. It was Renard, the man that Smith had hired to lead the party from The Dalles to the Barlow Road. The man Marcus Weiss caught stealing. The man Marcus Weiss whipped.

The other men had left and the camp was virtually defenseless.

Anderson saw Hezekiah Smith with a rifle in his hand. He was trying to get the thing loaded. Renard sprang on him, wrestling the rifle away. Then Renard went at the elderly man with a knife, brutally slashing at him until Hezekiah fell to the ground.

An Indian grabbed one of Walter Brown's daughters around the throat, dragging her toward the woods.

One of the white men had a club and he used it to bash a woman in the head.

Luisa Weiss ran from the camp. She had a child's hand in each of her hands. Her other child was running behind but falling away as the woman dragged the two children. Renard gave chase to the four of them and caught the child that was falling behind. Anderson watched him run the child through with the knife. Luisa Weiss had turned in time to see it, too, and she screamed, releasing her other children and running back for the child Renard had stabbed.

Enraged, and sickened by what he'd witnessed, Anderson charged at Renard. He had his rifle in the air like a club. Renard saw him coming and turned and ran toward the woods. About the time he reached the child's body, Anderson gave up his pursuit.

Beth Gordon picked up Hezekiah's rifle. She pulled the ramrod from the barrel and held the rifle to her shoulder. She swept the camp with the rifle until she saw one of the attackers straddling Jeb Smith's wife, tearing away the blouse she wore. Mrs. Gordon pulled the trigger and through the cloud of smoke saw the bullet smash into the man's chest. He heaved and fell away from Mrs. Smith, but then he struggled to his feet and ran into the woods.

ALFRED NORTON AND HIS sons were among the few men left at the camp when the others went off to catch John Gordon and Jeb Smith's sons. It hadn't been on purpose, but Norton was probably the best among them to leave behind.

Norton was forty-two-years-old and a veteran. The second day after the Townes Party crossed the Missouri River into Kansas Territory, they encountered a column of cavalry from Fort Leavenworth. The men were talking about war with Mexico and said they expected to soon be sent south to fight. Norton struggled with a decision that day. Should he reenlist and go fight or go on with his plans to settle in Oregon Territory. His wife was livid at the talk of it, and made the decision for him. His four sons ranged in age from twenty to the youngest at fourteen. Even the youngest boy was tall for his age and thick with muscle. Norton left his wife and two oldest boys at his father-in-law's farm in Illinois back in '32 to join the militia and fight the Sauks and Kickapoos under Black Hawk.

He'd not seen much fighting, just a pursuit and brief skirmish with a band of Sauks who'd raided a village in upper Illinois. The rest of the time, Norton's militia unit rode the countryside and camped and drank too much at the campfires.

Norton liked the life of the militia. When the Black Hawk war came to an end and the militia were sent home, Norton stayed at his father-in-law's with his wife just long enough to add another boy to his family, and then he enlisted in the regular army.

He spent a year at Fort Leavenworth, riding patrols along the Santa Fe Trail. There wasn't as much whiskey, but he enjoyed the life pretty well.

When his father-in-law died, Norton went back to work his wife's family farm.

He'd never found as much enjoyment in driving a plow. The closest he came was taking his boys hunting, which he did with all of them the moment they were old enough to carry and load a rifle.

They'd been applying grease to the axle of their wagon and another when the attack came.

Norton's oldest boy, Isaiah, won out in a fight to the death with one of the first Indians to charge from the woods. The two youngest boys loaded rifles and stood by their mother, protecting her and their wagon.

Al Norton grabbed his cavalry sword from the wagon, and with his second oldest son at his heels, chased into the woods after one of the assailants who was dragging away one of Walter Brown's daughters. Norton caught the man and gave him a ferocious slash on the back. The man turned the girl loose, and that's when Norton's son fell on him with a knife, stabbing him several times in the chest.

Norton pulled the boy.

"He's dead Joshua," Norton said. "You've done for him. See to the girl."

The girl was Walter Brown's red-haired daughter. She was a stunning beauty, and when the Brown's joined the Townes Party back at Bridger's Fort, Joshua Norton was instantly in love. The girl seemed to reciprocate the feelings. Though Al Norton thought quite a bit of Elias Townes and the others in the wagon train, he'd decided to go with Jeb Smith when the party split purely for the affection his son felt for the girl. He'd regretted his decision since he made it. He'd formed good friendships with some of those men in the other wagon train. But his wife, who was always soppy about these things, had pressed him, saying what is the difference from one wagon train to another, until he at last relented.

But he regretted now more than ever joining Jeb Smith.

"Get her back to the wagons," Al Norton said.

Joshua took Helen Brown by the hand – both of them ignoring the blood drenching his hands – and rushed her back to the safety of his armed brothers. It was at that point that Joshua lost sight of his father.

But the attack was over now.

The chaos wasn't finished.

Women and children had run into the woods.

Some were crying. Others stayed silent and hid, waiting for another wave of the attack, not realizing it was over.

Luisa Weiss was on the ground wailing. Everyone thought this fresh fit was prompted by the memory of Angela Suttle's mutilated body, understandably compelled to her mind by this sudden attack. But then they realized that she was slumped over the lifeless body of one of her children.

Hugh Anderson stumbled through the camp like a man in a daze.

It was the Norton boys who finally began settling things. They collected the women and children hiding in the woods. They took an accounting of the casualties.

One of Walter Brown's daughters was missing, the fifteen-year-old with the dark hair. Her name was Marianne.

Hezekiah Smith was badly injured with terrible slices on his chest.

Jeb Smith's wife had a gash on her cheek where she'd been punched or struck with a war hammer, she couldn't say which it had been.

A young man named Oscar Stuart who traveled with his wife was dead. The survivors guessed he must have been among the first to be attacked when the assailants rushed from the woods. His young wife was also killed. They had no children, but Stuart spoke often of the big family they intended to have when they were settled in Oregon.

Jack Horne was also dead.

Some of the livestock, including some of the horses, had scattered during the attack.

"How many of you have said we had nothing to fear from the Indians?" Beth Gordon demanded. "Elias Townes swore to me that we should worry more about bears and wolves than we should about savages!"

"Ma'am, this wasn't no Indian attack," Hugh Anderson answered her.

"It certainly was! The man I shot was an Indian."

"Yes, ma'am. There was Indians among 'em, but white men, too. And that man Renard. The guide. He was with them."

None among them even realized that it was still raining.

Jeb Smith and his posse returned a short while later and found the people there tending to their wounded. Isaiah Norton and Hugh Anderson provided Smith and the others with an accounting of what happened. Anderson was the only one who could say with certainty that he'd seen Renard and that there were white men among the attackers. Between them Anderson and Isaiah Norton guessed that there'd been something between eight and twelve attackers.

"And my father's missing," Isaiah said.

"Nobody is to leave in pursuit of these men until we've had an opportunity to get ourselves organized and decide what is best to do," Smith announced to the rest of the party.

"They have my daughter," Walter Brown said angrily. "I must go after Marianne, even if I have to go alone."

"Not until we can organize ourselves," Smith said again. "Hear what I'm saying to you Walter. You still have a wife and two daughters at this camp. This attack this afternoon would never have happened if Gordon hadn't convinced my sons to go off with him half-cocked. If we'd all been here, there would have been no attack. And if there had been, it would have turned out quite a bit differently."

"You can't lay this at my feet," John Gordon said angrily.

"I'll lay it where it belongs," Smith answered him. "Nobody leave. We've got to make a decision what to do."

"We've got to go for my daughter," Walter said. "There can be no choice in that."

Jeb Smith shook his head. His eyes went over the camp. It seemed in disarray. Beth Gordon was trying to comfort Luisa Weiss who, for the second time today, sobbed uncontrollably. His own wife's cheek was split open, the side of her face bruised already. There were bodies – bodies of the dead! – that needed to be buried.

"I just need time to think of what's best to do," Smith said.

But time was beginning to run out. Dusk was already beginning to settle in. Any pursuit would have to wait for morning or be conducted at night.

And before he'd reached any decision, Al Norton came walking into camp leading a string of eight saddled horses.

"Whoever it was that attacked us, they won't get far without their horses," Norton said.

JEB SMITH LED THE burial party.

No one thought to bury the new dead with Angela Suttle's body. Instead, they buried the Weiss child, Jack Horne, and the Stuarts together.

Hezekiah Smith was in no shape to cut boards and fashion crosses, so no markers went atop the graves. Just piles of rocks over shallow graves. They buried the bodies about a hundred yards from where Angela Suttle was buried, off the road and down a hill.

They took the bodies of the attacker Anderson had shot and the man Isaiah Norton killed just as the attack began and dragged them down the hill even farther, unceremoniously rolling them over a cliff into a deep ravine where the wolves would find them. They gave the same treatment to the Indian Joshua Norton had killed in the woods.

"I ain't breaking my back digging through this tough soil for those men," Jeb Smith said.

While the burial party handled its unpleasant task, Hugh Anderson took a couple of the older boys and started rounding up the livestock.

Al Norton led a party consisting of Walter Brown, John Gordon, Luke and Jacob Suttle, and his son Isaiah, to go in search of Marianne Brown. They followed the path Renard and the other men had taken when they retreated into the forest.

But darkness was quickly coming, and Norton feared that they would soon be blindly pursuing dangerous men.

They knew they were on the right track, though, when they came across the body of one of the assailants. It was the man Beth Gordon had shot off of Jeb Smith's wife. The men left the body where they found it.

Back at camp, the men gathered around a fire, constantly feeding it, desperate to try to warm themselves as a soft rain continued to fall.

"They tied their horses about two hundred yards from the cliff, back over that ridge above us," Al Norton said. He indicated the ridge to their northwest. Then he pointed off to the northeast, in the direction where his posse had discovered the body of the man Beth Gordon shot. "When they fled from the camp, I think they must have gone off in that direction. Whether they did it by accident or not, I don't know, but they missed their horses. They probably topped the ridge half a mile or more away from the horses. With the girl as a captive, probably having to get themselves organized and figure out who was hurt and who was killed, they didn't get back to the horses as fast as I got to them. I figure they moved through the woods to find the horses, probably got turned around a good bit when they couldn't find them where they expected to. And now they've retreated somewhere to make camp and figure out what to do next."

Jeb Smith nodded his head. It all made sense the way Norton explained it, but he knew the man was only guessing at any of it.

"They won't move in the dark, even with a captive and knowing there's a chance we're going to pursue. They'll hunker down somewhere in the woods for the night."

Walter Brown, even in the firelight, looked ghostly pale. For the second time on this journey, one of his daughters had been taken captive. That first time it had been his oldest daughter Sarah, taken captive by the men who'd been hired to guide the wagon train back at Bridger's Fort. Elias and Zeke Townes saved Sarah. Now, with Marianne taken, he looked around at the other men standing at the campfire and did not see a savior. Who among these men would rescue his daughter? Certainly not Jeb Smith. Al Norton and his sons were the most likely among this group in a fight. John Gordon meant well, but he couldn't track and he wasn't smart enough to out-think his adversary. Jacob Suttle was desperate for revenge, and Luke, too, but these men couldn't organize a posse. They just wanted blood for blood.

Brown had been reluctant to leave the Townes Party. Luke Suttle had been, also. They both left more from a sense of loyalty than because they thought it was the best thing.

Brown listened to Al Norton, knowing this man was the only hope Marianne had.

"If it really was that man Renard that Hugh Anderson saw, we know they'll make for The Dalles. They're going to go back east. As thick as this forest is, they'll surely take the road. And as long as we have their horses, they won't travel fast. I would recommend at first light some number of us ride east on the trail. I'm thinking we're about four miles from that steep ridge we climbed a couple of days back. Maybe less? That ridge was above that muddy river. What was it?"

"The White River," Jeb Smith said.

"We should go back that far, to the White River, and then turn and sweep back this way. If we go on horseback, we should be to the river by noontime. At the river, we'll turn and make our way back here to the camp with men fanned out in the trees. We'll either find Renard and the other men or we'll find their camp. If it's their camp, we'll turn east again. We'll chase him all the way back to The Dalles if we have to. The man's a drunkard. He won't stay away from available liquor for long."

"How do you know he's a drunkard?" John Gordon asked.

"I searched his saddlebags," Norton said with a nod at the stacked saddles sitting nearby. "Liquor bottles in all those saddlebags. My guess is that after that whipping he took, Renard hurried back to The Dalles and collected some of his drunken friends. Ne'er-do-wells, drunkards, and thieves, all of them. Cutthroats, as we know all too well. He wanted revenge for that raw treatment he took from Mr. Weiss. So, wherever he picked them up, whether it was at The Dalles or somewhere else, he hurried back and got them and then probably took some old Indian hunting trail to catch up to us. This wasn't no Indian raid. Had it been, they would have taken more hostages from among the older children, and they'd have killed all the adults and all the very young. We'd be having a different conversation tonight if this had been an Indian raid. Mostly, we'd be talking about how we were going to get out of this forest alive."

"How many should ride back to the river in the morning?" Jeb Smith asked.

"I'll take Isaiah and Joshua with me," Norton said. "The three of us can handle it. If I can get one or two more volunteers, I'd be satisfied with that."

"So few?" Walter Brown asked.

"I just need a man or two to help us spread out through the woods. Maybe one more to lead our horses."

"So few?" Jeb Smith said. "Shouldn't you take more?"

"There's not but four of these men," Norton said.

"How can you be sure there's only four? From what Anderson told us, and the other survivors, there could have been more than a dozen of them attacking the camp."

"They had eight horses, so we know there was never more than eight of them," Norton said. "Four of them are dead."

"But the others said there were more –" Jeb Smith argued, but Norton cut him off.

"They come into the camp shouting and yelling and killing folks, of course the others thought there was more of them. Everything was confusion and folks running around. But count the horses yourself. Never more than eight, and four are killed. One by Anderson, one by Mrs. Gordon, and two by my sons."

"This is a pointless debate," Walter Brown interrupted. "Al says he wants two volunteers. I'm one of them. I'm going with the party to rescue Marianne."

Jacob Suttle started to speak, but Luke cut him off.

"No," Luke said. "We'll stay here and help protect the camp in case they come back."

"I'll join the posse," John Gordon said.

21

ELIAS TOWNES WOKE THE next morning hoping the rain would have quit overnight. He heard no pitter patter on his tent, but he found himself disappointed when he opened the tent flap. The morning started gray and drizzly. It wasn't raining hard, but the present conditions were hardly better than the day before. Everything was wet. Everything was gray. Everything was cold. And it was already light outside, so whatever else, the Townes Party would be getting a later start today than it had the previous day.

"We've slept too late," Elias told Madeline.

"It was a hard day yesterday," his wife said. "Everyone probably needed an extra half hour of sleep."

"We can sleep in Oregon City," Elias said.

But Maddie was right. As the camp began moving in the gray morning, every chore seemed to take twice as long. Dry firewood became a problem, and the emigrants had to suffice with wet wood. But that meant campfires took longer to light and get burning. The oxen moved slow as the men tried to get their wagons hitched.

Seeing that the wagons wouldn't be moving any time soon, Elias saddled Tuckee. Cody Page was nearby, taking down Sophie Bloom's tent.

"Cody," Elias called to him. "Go and tell Zeke and Henry Blair to saddle their horses. You can saddle one for yourself too, if you want. I'm going to ride ahead and have a look at the road before we start out."

"Sure thing, Mr. Townes," Cody said. He finished with the tent and then went to find Henry and Zeke. In a short while, the four of them rode out of camp to scout ahead to get an idea of what the road looked like for the day's march.

The slope down the back side of the hill they'd climbed the previous day was treacherously steep. In the worst spots, it curved to take the descent at an angle to the slope and then curved back again, and a third time before finally reaching the bottom. Here, though, the land leveled out some.

"Once we're down this hill, we'll have an easy go of it for a while, it seems," Elias predicted.

If they'd climbed a thousand feet the day before, the drop down the other side only took them about four hundred feet.

But it was at the bottom of the slope, where the road ran relatively straight for some distance, that Cody Page spotted the riders coming toward them.

"Mr. Townes," Cody said. "There's riders up ahead."

And then one of the approaching riders shouted, "Is that Elias Townes?"

Elias gave Tuckee a touch on the shoulder with his knee, and the horse trotted forward. Zeke and Henry Blair followed him at a trot. When they came where Elias could better see the approaching riders, he realized it was Norton and some of the others from Jeb Smith's party. The riders all reined in and sat their horses facing each other.

"Mr. Brown?" Zeke said. "You don't look well. Is everything all right?"

"We've had some trouble," Al Norton said. "You don't know how glad I am to have come across you. Is the rest of the party with you?"

"They're breaking camp up the hill there," Elias said, tossing his head back on his shoulder.

Norton nodded his head.

"We come up that hill first thing in the morning a couple of days back. Made it another two miles or so back yonder, made camp there."

Elias nodded, hoping Norton would come to his story of their troubles.

"We ain't moved from that camp. Not yesterday, and we won't today. You'll overtake us if you get rolling out this morning."

"What trouble have you encountered?" Elias asked, feeling anxious that there might be something up ahead that would also delay his wagon train.

"My daughter's been taken," Walter Brown cut in. "Some others killed. Jacob Suttle's wife tortured and mutilated."

Brown's voice cracked at the words.

"Indians?" Henry Blair asked.

"Not entirely," Norton answered. "Some white men. Some Indians. We think they're led by that man we hired to guide us from The Dalles to the start of the road."

"Renard?" Zeke asked, remembering his supper with the man and the man's injuries.

"We had some unpleasantness with him after he got us to the gatehouse," Norton said. "Marcus Weiss caught him stealing and gave him a whipping for it. He run off at that point, but it seems he was determined to pay us back. And they done it in a bad way."

"Angela Suttle was killed?" Elias said.

"Her and some others. One of the Weiss children, that Horne boy who was packing west. Oscar Stuart and his wife, too."

"But our priority now is Marianne Brown," John Gordon cut in. "She was taken from the camp and we're hoping to find her before –" Gordon cut his eyes at Walter Brown. "Well, we're hoping to find her before they get too far."

Elias cut his eyes at Zeke. Zeke gave a reluctant nod to his head.

"How can we help?" Elias asked.

"I got Renard's horses," Norton said. "Him and the others with him are on foot. We reckon there's four of them, seeing as how I took eight horses from the woods and we killed four of his party defending ourselves. If you wanted to help in the search for the girl, it might mean finding her a bit quicker. And, of course, we'd be grateful."

Elias nodded his head.

"We'll help," he said. His eyes fell on his brother as Ezekiel seemed to have a knack for this sort of thing. "Zeke?"

"You say they attacked you at your camp?" Zeke asked. "And your camp is two miles ahead?"

"That's right," Norton said. "About two miles."

Zeke twisted in his saddle and looked at the hill behind them.

"What time did they attack you? When did you last see them?"

"An hour or so before dusk," Norton said.

Zeke nodded his head.

"They couldn't have come up the road in the night," he said. "Not and come past our camp without the night watch knowing they were there. And they wouldn't have tried that hill off the road in the dark. I would bet they're still somewhere in this valley."

"I would agree with that," Norton said. "They might have walked the road at night, but like you said, someone at your camp would have seen them on the road. And it would be too dangerous in the dark to get off the road, especially up on the sides of that hill."

Zeke let out a heavy breath as he gave a moment's thought.

"Elias, why don't you take these men and ride back up and let the folks at camp know. You can organize a posse. Start back down the hill, checking the woods. They'll try to hide from you, but if you come on foot and spread out, you can probably flush them out. Just like dove hunting."

Elias nodded his head.

"All right."

"Mr. Brown, can you take me, Cody, and Henry back to your camp and show me where you last saw these men?"

"I never saw them," Brown said helplessly. "I was away from camp when they attacked."

Zeke looked at Norton.

"My sons can show you where they fled after the attack," Norton said. "The two younger boys are at camp with their mother."

"That's good enough," Zeke said. "Mr. Brown, why don't you lead the way? We'll see if between us, me and Henry can't pick up the trail and give chase to Renard and the others."

"I'd rather stay with these men," Brown said. "I want to be with them when they find my daughter."

Zeke nodded his head.

"I understand that, but Walter, I don't think you're in any shape to help a posse. You ride on back with me." Zeke gave a grin at Elias. "Besides, I'd wager good money that Henry and I will be the ones to find her. And we'll bring her home to you at your camp faster than if you're out here kicking at bushes with these boys."

"Maybe I should ride with you," John Gordon said.

"No. I think Henry and I will be okay on our own."

"THIS MUST BE WHERE Norton found their horses," Zeke said.

The rain had made the tracks easy to follow. The bed of pine straw in the forest complicated things a bit, but here and there they found footprints in mud that kept them on the right track.

Zeke, Cody, and Henry left their horses with Hugh Anderson. They armed themselves, Zeke with his rifle and Colt Paterson, Henry and Cody with just a rifle each. All three men, though, carried long fighting knives.

Renard and his group had fled the camp with their captive and taken the easiest route. The forest, the lay of the land, naturally fed them toward a draw. They'd been at the run through here, and there were plenty of footprints to lead the three in pursuit.

Renard had followed a steep draw for some distance. Henry found marks where at least one of the men had lost his footing and slid in the mud. At the bottom of the draw, they came to a narrow canyon. The north side of it was a near vertical climb two hundred feet or more that would take them up toward Mount Hood. The climb ruled out them going any farther in that direction. Zeke guessed they'd have cut back to the west to try to find their way to their horses.

The three followed the canyon maybe half a mile. The canyon bottom was soft with the recent rain, and they found several footprints that confirmed Zeke's guess. An empty liquor bottle suggested that the men had spent the night there in the canyon.

"The fact that Marianne Brown's body ain't laying here beside this liquor bottle is probably the best news of the day," Zeke told Cody and Henry. "We can guess this is where they woke up this morning. At this point, they're going to try to get back to their horses. Norton's son said that Norton found the horses in the woods west of the camp. So, Renard and his men are going to have gotten up this morning and tried to get up this slope to get to their horses. We're looking for any sign of where they climbed out of this canyon."

They continued west – or roughly west – in the canyon until it opened wide to the south, an easy hill offering a way out of the canyon.

"I reckon this is where they climbed out of the canyon," Cody said.

"I expect so," Zeke agreed.

They took the hill but didn't find any sign that they were still on the trail. They went slow, painfully slow, until Henry spotted a patch of gray clouds through the canopy.

"The forest opens up ahead," Henry said.

The three men hurried forward and found themselves out on the Barlow Road. Zeke guessed they were probably a mile and a half or two miles west of Smith's camp.

Fresh footprints on the road made it easy to follow Renard's path, now.

Renard or one of the others had marked the place on the road where they hid their horses. They'd uprooted a two-foot pine sapling and hung it from the branch of another tree. Anyone else probably wouldn't have noticed it, but Renard and his men would have been looking for it. Zeke didn't see it until he realized that the muddy tracks left the road here.

A hundred yards or so into the woods, they came to a small clearing, the pine straw churned when eight horses had been tied here.

"So they came here this morning, looking for their horses, and found them gone. What did they do next?" Zeke said.

"Killed the Brown girl," Cody suggested.

"That seems likely, don't it?" Zeke said. "She'd be slowing them down, and they'd have to be worried about pursuit. And they're right here – close to Jeb Smith's camp. They'd feel the noose tightening right now. But we still don't have Marianne Brown's body, so maybe she's alive. Maybe they're thinking about selling her to someone."

Zeke chewed his lips while he thought about.

"Hell. I know where they are. Come on."

Zeke ran through the forest, holding his rifle in one hand out in front of him, leaping fallen branches and trees. Henry kept up, but just barely. He was surprised to see that Zeke could keep his breath running and leaping like this. Cody fell behind. He could swing and ax all day, or saw boards. But running wasn't part of his daily regimen. As Zeke and Henry outdistanced him, Cody slowed his run to a quick walk. Fortunately, they weren't going far.

After a few minutes, they came out of the woods with Jeb Smith's camp in sight. Only then did Zeke stop running, and now he was breathing heavy. Henry had fallen quite a ways behind him, and he struggled even more to catch his breath.

Their sudden appearance had startled the other emigrants. One of the women let out a gasp at the sight of them, another shouted her surprise. A couple of the men reached for nearby rifles, but then realized it was Zeke and Henry.

"Did you find anything?" Jeb Smith asked as Cody stepped over a fallen tree – one cut down by Barlow's road crew – out into the clearing of the camp.

"I think I know where they are," Zeke said, still breathing hard. "Cody, Henry, go get your horses saddled."

ZEKE DIDN'T SPEAK TOO loudly. The three men trotted their horses some distance before slowing them to a walk.

Cody noted that Zeke was watching the ground closely as they walked the horses, and periodically his eyes would land on something and he'd nod to himself.

"We're heading west, Zeke," Cody said.

Zeke chuckled but kept his voice low.

"Thanks for that, Cody."

"Didn't they say they figured Renard would make for The Dalles? That's back east."

"There's more than one way to get to The Dalles," Zeke said. His eyes roved the road again, and when they stopped, Zeke pointed to a spot just up ahead. "See it?"

Cody craned his neck to look past his horse's head.

"Is that another footprint?"

"It is," Zeke said. "I've seen maybe a couple dozen fresh tracks. When they saw their horses were gone and knew they'd have to get past Smith's camp to go east toward The Dalles, Renard and the others decided to go west instead. They knew that they'd have to go past Smith's camp, but they also knew they'd have to go past our camp. And they knew there was a good likelihood that we would already be alerted to the attack on the Smith Party."

"How did they know about us?" Henry Blair asked.

"I saw them a few nights ago, back when we were camped on the White River," Zeke said. "I saw something in the woods. I didn't know who it was.

I thought it might have been someone from Smith's Party, or Indians. I didn't think anything more about it, but now I'm convinced it was Renard and his group. They saw us at the White River. They knew we were close behind Smith. They had every reason to believe it wouldn't just be Smith's party scouring the woods for them, but us, too. And without horses, they couldn't hope to stay ahead of us. And they would know we'd go east looking for them because Renard had to figure he'd been recognized."

"So, turn west," Cody said, nodding his head. "Make for Oregon City. Stay ahead of the wagon trains, go the opposite direction we'd expect them to go."

"Raft back to The Dalles or take the livestock trail back, either way," Zeke said.

"How far up ahead of us do you think they are?" Henry Blair asked.

"Not far."

The riders came to a bridge over a deep ravine with a creek running down in the bottom of it. The ravine wasn't particularly wide, but without the bridge a wagon wasn't getting across it. If there'd been any doubt about whether or not they were still on the right track, the wet footprints on the wood removed them.

"Five people," Zeke said, dropping down from his horse and getting a close look at the prints. "And look at how small these prints are. That's Marianne Brown, still alive and walking. What? Maybe an hour ago?"

Across the bridge, the three riders kept their thoughts to themselves. They all felt it now, that they had to be close.

Half a mile after crossing the bridge, maybe a bit farther on than that, the three riders came around a bend in the road, and up ahead, about a hundred and fifty yards beyond them, they saw the four men and the kidnapped girl walking away from them in the middle of the road.

22

Zeke held up a hand to stop the other two men.

"Cody, you come with me. Henry, you stay here with the horses. Load your rifle and be ready to shoot if you have to."

The three of them dismounted.

The wind cut through the tops of the pines and spruce and firs. The light drizzle seemed to just hang in the air, but it muffled every sound as all three men drew their rifles and loaded them.

Two white men, an Indian, and Renard. Marianne Brown walked on the outside of the group. Renard had hold of her wrist. Zeke's attention shifted constantly from his work loading the rifle to the men down the road, just to be sure they didn't look back and know what was coming.

"When we get close, so close we won't miss, you shoot the man on the far left. Kill him if you can, maim him if you can't kill him. But don't miss him," Zeke said, shooting a stern look at Cody Page.

"I ain't gonna miss him, Mr. Zeke," Cody grinned, confidence shining from his face.

"I'll shoot the one next to him," Zeke said. "We'll shoot at the same time. Then we rush the other two. Drive into them hard. Knives. Fists. The butt of your rifle. Whatever gets the job done, but we put them down fast. Kill them, save the Brown girl."

Cody nodded his head and glanced at the men walking yonder.

"We'll save her," Cody said.

They didn't run. Zeke didn't want Cody to take a shot out of breath. But they had a pretty fast clip to their walk. Those in front of them straggled. They seemed exhausted. One of them, one of the white men, he seemed to be limping.

A couple of times, Zeke couldn't stand it so he jogged on ahead. The men with Marianne Brown went out of sight behind a curve. Zeke looked back and saw that Henry was leading the horses forward but keeping at a distance.

He jogged again. They reached the bend where the men had disappeared, and as they came around it, Zeke expected to see the backs of his quarry walking away from him.

Instead, they were stopped in the road. At a glance, Zeke could see what had happened.

Marianne Brown had fallen to the ground. Probably too exhausted to keep going. Renard had her by the wrist with both hands and was dragging at her, trying to get her to her feet. One of the white men had his hand on his knife, like he was about to deal with the problem of the girl who refused to go farther.

Trouble was, Marianne Brown had her back to Zeke and Cody Page, but the four men were all facing them as they came around the bend in the road. Zeke slid to a stop and felt Cody coming up behind him and then stop himself when he realized the situation.

For just a moment, the six men stood where they were, all of them looking at each other. The two almost as surprised to see the faces of the four as the four were to see the faces of the two. And in that moment, Zeke thought there was recognition in Renard's eyes. He remembered the man who'd fed him.

"Shoot," Zeke said.

"What?" Cody answered him.

Zeke pulled back the hammer as he threw his rifle to his shoulder. "Shoot!"

Zeke squeezed the trigger and the cap snapped, but with no corresponding belch of smoke, no thundering bark. No bullet sailing down range to drop one of the men. Wet powder.

Cody fired his rifle. The smoke clung to the drizzly rain and hung there in front of them, blinding Zeke for just a moment. But saw the white man with his knife in his hand stagger, stumble back, and fall over, the knife on the ground now and both of his hands clutching at his stomach. He let out a shout of surprise, maybe pain.

"He shot me!" the man called out.

Zeke tossed his rifle to the side of the road and rushed at the three remaining men. Cody page twirled his rifle, and cocked it over his head, gripping the barrel with both hands. He charged with Zeke.

As he charged forward, Zeke drew the Colt Paterson from its holster and thumbed back the hammer. The trigger dropped from the belly of the gun, and Zeke fired a shot from the hip and thought he'd hit one of the men. The man was an Indian and wore breeches of deerskin, but he wore an overcoat, much too large for him, with what appeared to be a quilt sewn into it as a lining. The man jerked like he'd been shot by Zeke's bullet, but Zeke couldn't take the time to be sure.

Renard had fetched a rock hammer from his belt, and he reached high up over his head with the thing. At first Zeke thought he intended to defend himself with it – and Zeke didn't doubt that he would – but then Zeke realized that he intended to use the hammer on Marianne Brown. He was looking at her and dragging her by the armpit up off the ground. He was getting her head in a position to crush her skull.

Zeke threw himself bodily into Renard. He drove his shoulder toward the man's throat.

The two of them fell to the ground, Zeke almost lying atop Renard. As they went down, Zeke lost his grip on the Colt. He felt Renard's hammer come down on his back, but the awkward angle had taken all the force from the blow, and Zeke carelessly shook it off.

He grabbed Renard's wrist, holding him fast so that he couldn't take another swing. Zeke straddling the man now. Renard fought back. He wrestled to get his hand free. But Zeke found himself to be significantly stronger than the halfbreed Indian. Renard couldn't even twist to try to protect himself, to try to shield his face and chest with his shoulder. Zeke had him pinned there in the muddy road.

And with all the strength built up from years of swinging axes and pushing saw blades, Zeke smashed a fist into Renard's face. That one punch took most of the fight out of the man. Zeke pressed a hand on Renard's chest to push himself up from the ground, and then he dragged Renard with him. Still holding him by the wrist, Zeke half-carried, half-dragged Renard away from the girl, toward the pines on the side of the road.

He was like some kind of rag doll, flaccid and feeble.

Zeke bashed Renard in the side of the head with his forearm and then wrenched the hammer from his hand and gave him a terrible bashing with it. Two, three shots to the head, busting open his skull like a melon.

Renard fell lifeless to the ground at the base of the pine.

Cody was dealing similarly with the other white man. Cody lacked some of Zeke's height, but he was broad in the shoulders and chest. Elias had once joked that they could save money on oxen by yoking the Page brothers to one of the wagons.

Cody had his knife in his hand and it was already scarlet as Zeke watched him drive it into the man again. Cody shoved the man to the ground and gave him a kick. He coughed blood and tried to drag himself to his feet, but he collapsed again. He was choking on his own blood.

Zeke sought the Indian he'd shot with the Colt and found him fleeing west down the road. He was running, but his run was awkward, as if he was trying to run with one leg and not making much headway. Zeke rushed at the man. He'd gone only ten or fifteen yards. Zeke raised the stone hammer into the air and as he caught up to the Indian, he swung the hammer at the man's head like he was felling a tree.

One chop cracked the man's skull.

Zeke ran past him and then turned on him. He gave the hammer another swing at the man's head, but it was unnecessary. Three of the four men lay dying on or beside the Barlow Road. The fourth – that was the first man Cody shot. He'd been out of the fight from the moment it started, but he'd not been killed outright by Cody's rifle shot.

Zeke looked back to Cody, and that's when he saw that fourth man, clutching at his wounded belly with one hand, push himself up from the ground with the other.

His whole body was bent as he came up off the ground, his back arced like a stone bridge over a creek. As the man stood up, still hunched, but on two feet now, Zeke realized he held in his hand the knife he'd dropped when Cody shot him.

"Cody!" Zeke shouted.

But his warning came too late. The man stumbled two or three steps and then used the last of his energy to throw himself at Cody. Cody twisted at Zeke's warning, and the white man's knife plunged into his side.

Zeke rushed at the man, but he'd already fallen away into the mud.

Cody held his arm at an awkward angle and stood for a moment looking at the handle of the knife sticking out of his side.

"Oh, Mr. Zeke, that ain't good," Cody said. His face went pale and he reached out a hand like he'd gone suddenly dizzy.

Marianne Brown sat in the mud watching all this transpire. Not a word or a scream or a sob escaped her. Zeke went to the Colt Paterson he'd dropped and picked it up from the ground. He walked over to the man Cody had shot and stood over him, the Colt aimed right at the man's face.

"Do it," the man snarled.

Zeke squeezed the trigger, but the percussion cap must've come off when he dropped the gun. The hammer fell with a lackluster click. He cocked back the hammer again and saw the cap on the next nipple. The man on the ground, he'd lost his venom. His eyes grew wide as he watched the cylinder on the Colt turn. Zeke squeezed the trigger. The heavy gun bounced in his hand as it thundered its report, and the man on the ground went rigid for just a second before he fell limp.

"Cody?" Zeke said.

Cody Page still struck an odd pose. His right arm high in the air, held over his head so as not to hit the knife handle sticking out of his side. His left arm was out like a bird's wing steadying him so he didn't fall over.

"I'm all right," Cody said. "I just gotta get this out of me."

He reached with his left hand for the knife handle. Zeke didn't know enough to stop him. Cody pulled the long blade out of his side, and like water held back by an earthen dam crumbling before its weight, the blood poured from the wound.

"Sit down, Cody," Zeke said.

Quickly, Zeke stripped his shirt from his back, bunched it into a ball and pressed it hard into Cody's side, trying to get the blood to stop.

Cody was sitting in the road now, growing paler by the second.

"I need to lie down," he said, his breath hardly coming to him.

"Okay, Cody. You can lie down."

"Not here. I don't want to die in the mud."

"You're not going to die, Cody," Zeke said. But his shirt was red with blood now, and it was dripping from the shirt.

"Help me over to the woods there, Zeke."

Zeke had to lift the man and drag him, but he managed it, getting Cody off the road. He put him down as gently as he could. Cody looked straight up at the canopy of the enormous pines and spruce trees.

"Damn if there ain't a lot of nice trees here, Zeke. You and Elias picked a good spot."

23

Henry Blair helped Zeke wrap Cody's body in Cody's horse blanket, and they put his body over his horse's back. Zeke helped Marianne Brown onto his horse, and he walked back. It was nearly dark when they arrived back at Jeb Smith's camp.

The Brown family's celebrations at the return of their daughter were muted when they saw the state she was in. Zeke didn't press her with many questions and didn't know what sort of torture she might have endured at the hands of those men who took her. He knew she might never recover. She never acknowledged her rescue or the man who died trying to save her, but that didn't bother Zeke. What could he expect from a girl who'd endured so much?

At the camp, they found Zeke a shirt to put on. He was half frozen after walking back in the rain without his shirt and his coat caked in mud and sopping wet. They found blankets for both him and Henry. Beth Gordon put cups of hot coffee in their hands, and Zeke did feel a little revived drinking it in front of a campfire.

Henry told most of the story for Zeke. He told them how they'd tracked the men, followed them down the road. He didn't have the details of the fight, but that wasn't important anyway. He had the major points. Four bad men were killed on the road. And one good one. And one girl was saved.

By the time Henry had told the story and answered questions to everyone's satisfaction, darkness was upon them.

"You can stay the night here," Jeb Smith offered.

"I appreciate it, Jeb. Honestly. But I'd just like to get back to my family."

Smith had sent Hugh Anderson on horseback to find the men searching the road back to the east and to let them know the girl was recovered. And now those men rode into camp, all of them holding torches.

It was Norton and his sons and John Gordon from Smith's Party. It was Elias and Jerry Bennett and Johnny Tucker and Captain Walker and Caleb Driscoll from the Townes Party

"Zeke, you look like hell," Elias said, standing over his brother at the campfire.

"Can I speak with you for a moment, Mr. Townes?" Jeb Smith said to Elias.

"Certainly."

The two men walked away from the others, out to the edge of the camp where only the faintest of light reached their faces.

"We're in bad shape here, Mr. Townes," Smith said. "We've lost women and children and men. I've got families that are devastated now. We're all cold and wet and miserable. The Brown girl? I don't know that her mind will ever recover from whatever horrors were inflicted upon her, but I know she won't be better before we reach Oregon City. We lost the Cayuse we hired to drive our stock, and the Horne boy. And I can tell you for a fact, half the men in my party wish they'd never joined with me and stayed with you instead. Norton? Poor Mr. Brown. Jacob Suttle has been glaring his hate at me all afternoon. I think he blames me for what happened to his wife. And someone told me Hugh Anderson is planning to ask if he can rejoin your party."

"He asked when he came to fetch us just now," Elias said. "I told him he'd be welcome but that you could probably use the help."

Smith nodded his head.

"Here's what I'd like to ask," Smith said. "Can we join your wagon train? I don't mean you do any work for us. But I mean, would you mind if we just travel along behind you? We'll all handle our own, and my boys and I will do double the work if we have to help these folks. But we ain't had much luck, and I'm worried at the next obstacle we might never reach Oregon City."

Elias clenched his jaw and took a few deliberate breaths.

He felt some anger toward Jeb Smith. It had been a strike against Elias's pride to have Smith lead a revolt in the wagon train.

But Elias nodded now.

"Can you find Jerry and Johnny a dry place to sleep tonight if I leave them here?" Elias said.

"Of course we can."

"Then I'll have them stay here. Come morning, they'll do what they need to do to help you get your livestock rounded up, yoke up them oxen and get your teams hitched. If it's what you want, you can ride behind us when we pass your camp tomorrow. If you'd prefer, you can just merge into the middle of the wagon train and we'll go on as before like nothing ever happened. Jerry and Johnny can help to get your livestock in with our livestock. That way you don't have to worry about how you drive them separate from ours with not enough hands to do it."

"That's more than kind of you," Smith said. "It's a generosity I don't deserve. But I'm swallowing my own pride even asking, trying to do what's right for these people."

Elias gave a small chuckle.

"It's no easy task being a wagon train captain."

"No," Smith said. "It's a lot easier being in the body of the wagon train and thinking you know better than the man leading it."

"Nothing more needs to be said about it," Elias said. "We'll rejoin the group tomorrow. But I'd better see to Zeke now, and I need to get back and tell Will what's happened to his brother."

Alfred Norton found the two men and walked over to them. He'd talked to Zeke and gotten the story of the rescue.

"Mr. Townes, I'd like to have a word with you," Norton said stiffly. "And it's good that you're here, too, Mr. Smith, because you should also hear what I have to say. Mr. Townes, I'm humbly, hat-in-hand, asking if you'll let me buy back into your wagon train. I made a bad error in judgment when I decided to join with Mr. Smith. You know my boy, Joshua?"

"Mr. Norton," Elias said. "It's all right. You don't have to say anything more."

"No. I want it to be said and to be out in the open. My boy, Joshua? He's sparked on Walter Brown's daughter, and against my better judgment, I said we could join this wagon train so he wouldn't have to be separated from her. That was a foolish mistake on my part. I abdicated my most important responsibility – the safety of my children – in favor of the whims of a teenage boy. I don't expect any special favors, and I'll buy in with what I took out back at the mission."

Elias held up a hand to stop Norton.

"Mr. Norton, it's fine. All y'all will be back with us tomorrow. Mr. Smith and I have just been talking, and we agreed that considering your losses, it just makes more sense for our two parties to come together tomorrow and finish out the journey as one wagon train."

"Who'll be leading it?" Norton asked.

Elias chuckled.

"After coming this far, I don't know that the wagon train needs a captain, Mr. Norton. Everyone should know what they have to do by now. But if there's a decision that needs to be made, I'll consult with Mr. Smith and we'll reach a conclusion together."

It was a lie, mostly. Elias had no intention of consulting with Jeb Smith about anything. But it was a lie to spare the man's dignity, and Elias figured that was a decent thing to do.

Sophie Bloom wept when she heard the news.

Will Page took it without much visible emotion, but Elias and Zeke both knew that Will was torn up inside.

"He died a good man's death," Zeke said to Cody's brother. "He was saving that girl. He traded his life for hers, and there's only honor in that, Will."

"Yes, sir, Mr. Zeke," Will said. "I reckon. But I'd rather he be a shameful sonuvabitch and still be here."

"Uh-huh. Me, too, Will."

With the morning sun shining on them they buried Cody Page at the top of the ridge.

To the north, the glacial peak of Mount Hood stood within sight of the grave. A man looking south could see the hills and spurs rolling away from the enormous Cascade mountain. The hills and spurs covered in trees.

"Cody would have approved of this spot," Will said. "If I had every day for the rest of my life, I'd never be able to count all the trees out there. Cody would like that."

Zeke gave Will a clap on the shoulder, and the two men made their way down to the camp where the wagon train was just beginning to move.

They'd finally make the descent down off the ridge and then it would be level ground to Smith's camp.

The descent required brakes and locked wheels. Henry and Elias and Zeke and several other men rode close to the wagons just in case one started to get away from them. On the curves in the road, Elias held his breath several times thinking a poorly loaded wagon was about to topple, but they didn't lose a single one.

At the bottom of the slope, Elias stopped the train to change out the oxen. The steep slope had been a difficult burden on those pulling the wagons, and Elias figured they'd get more out of the rest of the day if they used fresh teams.

Some of the folks grumbled some about the stop. Changing out the teams was a chore no one looked forward to. But everyone did what Elias told them to do. If nothing else, he finally felt like he'd garnered their trust.

They reached Smith's camp at midday. Having sent Henry Blair ahead, Smith was ready for them. The Smith Party's wagons rolled into the wagon train seamlessly, and the families who'd traveled two thousand miles together greeted each other like they'd never been apart. A few people held some ill will toward Smith, but it quickly dissipated when they saw that he wasn't going to complain or try to stir trouble.

They left one wagon behind. Smith had asked a couple of the men to clear out the Stuarts' wagon. Provisions would be divided among the families. Valuables could be boxed up and sent back to Oscar Stuart's family in the East. Anything too big send back could be sold in Oregon City and the money sent to family.

By the close of the day, they'd made better than eight miles from Smith's camp, mostly traveling through a reasonably level valley between big hills north and south of them.

They camped at a spot near a tall, narrow waterfall. Everything was wet and green and the rocks around the waterfall were slick. Mothers worried and followed their small children around and fathers told their older children to keep a watch on the little ones.

Zeke shook his head as Towser and Mustard played in the creek below the waterfall.

"Ain't that cold?" he asked their dogs, but their answer was to growl and snap and paw at each other in the middle of the stream.

No one knew how to treat those families who had suffered loss.

The men spoke bracingly to Jacob Suttle. They urged Luke to keep him busy once they arrived in Oregon City so that he didn't have time to think about it. Some of the women who'd become friends with Angela offered Jacob their sympathy, but they hardly knew what to say to him.

It was hardest to speak to the Weiss family.

Marcus Weiss had spent two thousand miles trying to keep his family secluded. He didn't like for his children to play with the other children. He domineered his wife so that she hardly made friends beyond pleasantries in passing.

While the others spent the last bit of the afternoon enjoying the waterfall, Marie Townes noticed Luisa Weiss and her two surviving children were sitting at their wagon. Marcus was off collecting firewood.

"Why don't I take the children to the stream to let them play with the others?" Marie said.

"I don't think Mr. Weiss would approve," Luisa said.

The woman's eyes were red from crying, but it was the blackened eye that concerned Marie. She did not know if Luisa had earned that when the wagon train was attacked or she'd received it from her husband. Mrs. Norton had told Marie how Weiss had struck his wife across the face when she discovered Angela Suttle's body.

"Nobody is asking Mr. Weiss," Marie said. "Better yet, why don't you bring them to the stream with me?"

Marie reached out a hand and helped Luisa to her feet. Luisa offered a wan smile.

"Thank you," she said.

The two women took the children, and they joined in with some of the other children who were running and leaping over the stream. Luisa even laughed when her son jumped the stream and landed in some mud. She seemed to catch herself, but the next child to try to jump the stream, one of Wiser McKinney's boys, put a foot in the stream and shouted how cold it was. Marie laughed with her that time.

But no one had trouble speaking to Will Page.

A handshake. A clap on the back.

"I just wanted to say to you what a good man your brother was," folks said to him – men and women. Several of them shared a funny story, or a time Cody helped them along the trail.

Will was grateful for their memories of his brother.

No one offered sympathy to Sophie Bloom. Most didn't even realize how close she and Cody had become.

But Madeline found her sitting on a rock watching her children playing with the others.

"I've known Cody for years," Maddie said. "All these rough men who work for my husband, they come around the house and steal pies and force me to cook like I'm an army cook. They're all good boys. They live their lives with no fear, you know. Dropping trees that could smash them to bits. Climbing trees. Swinging axes. They're all just boys to me. That's how I think of them. But they're good men. Cody was one of the best of them, though. Always polite. Always the first one to help me. And my goodness, I've never seen him act like he did around you."

A tear rolled down Sophie Bloom's cheek.

"How do you mean, Mrs. Townes?" she asked.

"He was smitten with you is what I mean," Maddie said. "I don't know how much you and he talked or what you talked about. And I'm not prying. I don't need to know. But I wanted you to hear it from someone who has known Cody since he was still mostly a boy. I do think there was coming a day, probably not until after we reached Oregon City, when he would have asked you to be his wife."

Sophie swallowed hard.

"I thought very highly of Mr. Page," she said.

"I know you did," Maddie said, and she patted Sophie's knee.

24

ELIAS INTENDED TO SPEND a single night at the camp near the waterfall, but Jerry Bennett and Johnny Tucker, riding in search of forage for the livestock, found a vast meadow about a mile south of the camp. The animals hadn't had decent forage since they'd gotten on the Barlow Road, so Elias agreed to spend two full days there. It gave the ground some time to dry out after the rains they'd endured, and the animals needed their strength for this last push.

He didn't know for sure how far the Barlow Road went. Someone back at The Dalles had said it would be a hundred miles to Oregon City. Judging purely by the fact that they were now just a little southwest of the peak of Mount Hood, Elias figured they were about half that distance. If so, they were averaging about four miles a day. It was going to take them most of a month to make the last hundred miles of the trail.

When they finally broke camp at the waterfall, they only made it about two miles before Henry Blair rode back from scouting ahead to speak to Elias.

"I think we've reached Laurel Hill," Henry said.

From Strickland at the gate and from some of the people back at The Dalles, they'd heard the name Laurel Hill. It had been described to them as something to be feared. Someone had even said that Laurel Hill itself was enough to make them regret not rafting their wagons to Oregon City.

"How bad is it?" Elias asked.

"You can't even realize how bad it is until you see it," Henry said. "It's worse than that ridge we come down a couple days back."

"It's really that steep?" Elias asked.

"Yes, sir. I don't know how that Mr. Barlow can call this a road and charge people to come across it when a wagon ain't likely to make it from one side of the road to the other in one piece."

"Wagons have come down it in front of us," Elias said. "We'll lock wheels and use ropes to lower the wagons."

"No, sir, Mr. Elias. You don't understand."

With the trees so thick and no point from which they could look out, Elias had no concept of where they were in the mountains nor how steep the hill in front of him fell away. The heavy forest on both sides of the road constantly left the travelers blind to what came around the next bend.

With Henry leading him, Elias rode forward a ways on Tuckee to see for himself.

At the precipice of the hill, Elias dismounted and stood at the top. It was worse than the slope back in the Blue Mountains where they'd lost Jeb Smith's wagon.

"How far down, do you reckon?" Henry asked.

"Henry, I can hardly guess. A thousand feet? Two thousand? But it's not a descent. It's a drop."

"Yes, sir. I tried to tell you."

"We're standing at the top of a cliff."

Henry laughed. Elias was incredulous.

"A cliff with a lean," Henry said.

There at the top, where Barlow's road crew had cleared away trees, Elias had one of the best views he'd had yet of the spurs and hills rolling away down the side of Mount Hood. Miles of forested hills stretched out to the horizon, and Elias was sure that beyond the farthest big hill, or maybe the one after that, would be the Willamette Valley and Oregon City. But he couldn't see the valley. Not yet.

What he could see was about a hundred feet down the trail before the branches became too thick and blocked the view farther. It was no wider here than the width of a single wagon, and like the rest of the Barlow's road, Elias wondered if it was even that wide. But the way the pines grew at an angle from the side of the hill, Elias could tell that the hill wasn't going to level out for them.

"Another year or two of people coming down this road, and I've got a feeling our friend Mr. Barlow will be the most hated man in all of Oregon Territory," Elias told Henry.

Henry laughed again.

"Yes, sir. We ain't reached the bottom yet, and I can already tell you that I hate the man."

Some of the others were coming now on foot to see for themselves. The McKinney brothers. Jeb Smith. Captain Walker.

"This must not be the road," Wiser McKinney said, turning to look around to find their actual route.

"This is it," Solomon said. "Look at the marks on the trees. This is the way they've come before us."

"We'll be lowering the wagons again," Elias said. "And I reckon it's going to take more than just a few of us to do it. Every man's going to have to pitch in."

"Start passing the word that everyone will have to secure their loads," Captain Walker called back.

"No, sir, Captain Walker," Elias said. "We won't be securing the loads. We'll be toting everything down by hand. Nothing but empty wagons go down this hill."

The men were joined by others, and they stared down the impossible hill discussing how they would proceed. Several people had ideas, and most of them agreed that the best idea being they should search for some other way to the bottom of the hill.

Rope marks on the big pines told them what they'd have to do. They'd be lowering the wagons inch by inch. But there were also stumps showing where dozens of trees had been cut down at the top of the hill, and not for building the road. These stumps were a mystery until Jeb Smith provided the answer.

"Anchors," he said. He'd walked part of the way down the hill and discovered several places where big pine branches were stuck in the roadway. He'd kicked them away into the woods, but he'd remained puzzled by the branches. He kept walking until he reached the base of the hill, and there he saw the answer. Dozens of big pine trunks were discarded at the base of the hill. Then Smith made the arduous climb back to the top, just in time to answer the question. "They're cutting down these trees and tying them behind the wagons as anchors. The base of the hill is littered with pine logs sixty or eight feet long."

The Townes Party made camp at the top of Laurel Hill that night.

The next day, they spent the entire day carrying items down the hill. Sacks of flour and beans. The pioneers slid down the hillside their kegs of nails; they could not roll them for fear that they would get away and smash to bits at the bottom of the hill. They did the same with their casks of water.

Children toted blankets and kettles. Men toted pots and pans and tools. Women carried clothes and lanterns.

Men and women and teenagers all had to work. Everyone made three or four trips up and down Laurel Hill. Even the small children had to tote something down if they were old enough to walk and carry. Only those who were too old – Hezekiah Smith and Betty Carlisle – too young, or too pregnant – Sophie Bloom – made just one single trip down the hill. And for now, the three of them stayed at the top.

Every family member had to pitch in. Every family helped every other family. The job was too big to not help. They all suffered from scraped elbows and scraped knees. Almost no one among the party made the trek up and down Laurel Hill without at least once losing their footing on a loose rock or an exposed root or a slick spot of mud.

Mothers and fathers shook their head in dismay to see the way the younger children complained with every step going down the hill toting a blanket or some other light object and then ran and laughed the entire way up.

"It's too bad to have that much energy and not be able to pack them with heavier loads," Jefferson Pilcher said.

Elias and his men unloaded from his wagon every saw blade and ax, every sharpening file and cant hook, every sledgehammer and log splitter, every bark spud and drag saw and maul. All the tools came out and most had to be toted to the base of the hill. But they left a couple of saws and a few axes at the top, intending to try Jeb Smith's idea of using felled trees as anchors.

Jerry Bennett and the Tucker brothers and Caleb Driscoll and William Page dropped a couple of big pines and used the trunks to fashion rough sleds. The heavy items – mostly stoves but also a few dressers or cabinets

– were strapped to the sleds and lowered by rope in the same fashion that Elias intended to lower the wagons.

The entire morning was occupied with the individual treks down and back up Laurel Hill. But soon the piles of possessions at the top started to diminish. And then they had only the big things, the furniture and the stoves.

All the men pitched in on that. Even Jeb Smith who had no stove nor furniture, lent his back to the effort.

They lowered the stoves on the sleds about a hundred feet at a time. They'd wrap a rope a turn or two around a pine tree, tie it to the sled and lower it down the slope until they got to the end of the rope. Those men would hold fast while another team, a hundred feet lower, would tie their rope to the sled and untie the other. In this way, using the sleds and then dragging them back up the hill, the stoves and furniture got to the base of Laurel Hill.

Solomon McKinney, after climbing up Laurel Hill for the fourth time that morning, announced that from top to bottom, Laurel Hill was seventeen-hundred feet. If he'd said it was seventeen-thousand feet, not a single person in the party would have corrected him.

"My thighs are on fire," Zeke admitted.

"Think of how the rest of us feel," Elias told him. "You're in better shape than probably any of us."

Shortly after noontime, the women and children made their last journey down Laurel Hill. Then the men began taking the livestock down the trail. Even the horses had to be walked. They left a few oxen at the top of the hill to pull the wagons up to the precipice, but other than those, the rest went down. It was slow going. A lot of the bigger beasts refused to go and had to cajoled into it. And if they found a place that didn't make them feel dizzy part way down the hillside, they stopped and refused to go farther. The men employed harnesses and whips and shoulders and liberal amounts begging to get the animals down to the bottom.

If the Kentuckian Sam K. Barlow was cussed once on that day, he was cussed a thousand times.

In fact, some of the pioneers cussed every man who'd ever been born or set foot in Kentucky, knowing full well that the Townes brothers and all their men came from Paducah. But neither Elias nor Zeke nor any of the other Kentuckians in the party had any energy or strength to argue. On that day, they hated Barlow enough to hate Kentucky, too.

ZEKE TOWNES, CALEB DRISCOLL, and Johnny Tucker volunteered to be the first team to get Elias's wagon down the slope using a tree as an anchor.

They didn't have enough length of good rope to employ the block and tackle. If they wrapped a rope around a tree and lowered a wagon, they'd be changing out rope every hundred feet. In the entire wagon train, they had only one five-hundred foot length of rope that they'd trust to hold the weight of a wagon. They could do that, change ropes every hundred feet or so, but they'd be days getting all the wagons down the slope.

So Jerry and the others dropped a hundred foot pine and used the animals remaining at the top of the hill to drag it over to Elias's wagon. They used chains to attach the tree trunk to the wagon.

Elias put a pole in Johnny Tucker's hand.

"Don't step in front of that wagon," Elias said. "But walk beside it. If a rock holds up a wheel, you use the pole to nudge the rock out of the way."

Caleb Driscoll climbed onto the side of the wagon and stepped down on the brake shoe. Those brake shoes had a tendency to fail to latch onto the wheel, and it was Caleb's job to keep the brake shoe pressed onto the wheel.

"If we lose this wagon and it starts to go, you jump off," Elias said. "You'll get scraped up pretty good, but it's better than getting dead."

Zeke got into the wagon and held onto the brake.

"Brother. I've got nothing for you," Elias said. "If the wagon goes, you'll go with it. All you can do is hang on and ride the tornado."

"It's probably a good thing Marie is down at the bottom of the hill," Jefferson Pilcher chuckled.

It took two dozen men pushing on the wagon and dragging on the tree trunk to get the entire assembly started down Laurel Hill. The men all crowded together and watched as the wagon started to go. Zeke put his weight into the brake. Caleb Driscoll held the shoe in place. Johnny Tucker walked along with his pole in hand, occasionally nudging a rock. The tree anchor did its job, dragging behind the wagon and slowing its descent.

The ride down was more like a slow scraping over a washboard than a tornado, Zeke decided. By the time he reached the bottom, his fingers were sore from gripping the brake handle so hard. His arms ached. And felt like his bones had been rattled.

"My teeth hurt," Zeke said.

But they'd made it.

And now, behind them, the second wagon was beginning its descent.

Jerry Bennett kept a team dropping trees as fast as they could. Every time he dropped a tree, they were ready to send down the next wagon. After seeing four wagons go down successfully, Elias was willing to have two on the hill at the same time, but only if the crew in the second wagon had done it once already.

Zeke rode Laurel Hill six times. By the time he walked back up after the sixth wagon, he'd forgotten how many times he had gone up and down Laurel Hill, between taking down items and livestock and wagons.

Maddie and Marie organized the women and children at the base of Laurel Hill, and by dusk, with all of them working together, they had all the tents put up and the campfires burning. But more than half the wagons remained at the top of Laurel Hill. It was going to take another day to get the remainder of the wagons down. Jerry and his crew were exhausted. There was a day's work at the base of the hill. Everything had to be loaded back into the wagons and the loads secured.

It was a spent but grateful group of men who made their way to the base of Laurel Hill and found supper waiting on them.

Two more days were lost at Laurel Hill.

It took all of the next day to get the rest of the wagons down the hill. No man was available to load his wagon while that work was done. Everyone was needed.

The second day, the emigrants rested and loaded their wagons. It was hard work, especially for weary men, but it didn't compare to the work they'd done the previous two days.

The third day, the Townes Party got moving again.

The creek at the base of Laurel Hill tended to jump its banks. The recent rains didn't help, but Elias figured down in the bottoms here it probably never got dry. The oxen slugged through the mud. The wheels mired in it. Wagons got stuck and they had to cut levers to get them out.

Elias sent Henry Blair forward to scout, and Henry came back and said they had another mile and a half of mud to get through. They hadn't even gone a hundred yards from their camp. Some of the wagons hadn't moved yet.

"If Barlow was here right now, I'd shoot that man," Elias said, his anger boiling over. "This ain't a road. This is a flimflam, and Barlow is a fraud."

The emigrants unhitched their teams and went back to the base of Laurel Hill. With axes and saws, they began cutting down their anchors into five-foot lengths. They split the logs in two and used horses and oxes to drag each length to the worst spots of mud on the road.

The work took several hours, but by the afternoon the wagons had rolled out of the mire to higher ground.

25

THEY LEFT LAUREL HILL behind, and within a couple of days found themselves in a valley and traveling beside the Sandy River. Down in the valley, the ground was solid and flat, at least flatter than they'd seen in weeks, and Elias's parade of prairie schooners rolled over it with relative ease. The river valley stretched about a mile between two big mountain spurs that came down off of Mount Hood – the foothills of the Cascades. The hillsides were covered in spruce and pine and fir.

"I reckon this is what we come here for," Zeke said to Caleb Driscoll as they cut through the valley. "A couple of weeks and we'll be in these hills shaving them bald."

They camped about a mile west of the Sandy River.

If Elias had hoped that they'd encountered the last obstacle, he was quickly disappointed.

Henry had been scouting ahead when he rode back to say they were coming to a river crossing.

"There's a ford. I walked my horse across it. Got my boots wet, and the river is pretty swift."

Swift and deep enough to reach a horse's belly. That was deep enough to take a wagon downstream if it was running too fast.

Elias consulted his brochure, the pamphlet that had been his guide since the Missouri River. He didn't expect to find anything about this ford. They were on a route now that didn't exist when the pamphlet was published. But in looking at it, Elias did note something of interest.

He turned Tuckee around, too excited not to say something to Zeke.

"We're coming to a river crossing," Elias said. He handed Zeke the pamphlet, opened to a page that carried a map of the Willamette Valley.

"What am I looking for?" Zeke asked.

"I'm guessing we're right here," Elias said, pointing at the map to a spot west of Mount Hood. It didn't show the Barlow Road, and details on the maps were sparse. But it did show a river about where they were. "That means this here is the river we're coming to. Look at the name of the river."

Zeke squinted at it.

"The Clackamas," he said. He looked up at Elias, giving him a grin. "We're home."

"Damn close to it," Elias said. "Our timber lease is on the Clackamas River."

They strung a rope at the crossing. Actually three ropes, tied together. If a wagon got swept downriver by the current, Elias hoped the rope would catch the wagon. They were so close now that he didn't want to risk not getting every wagon to Oregon City. But they managed the ford without incident. Elias guessed from the map in the brochure that they were something close to ten miles from Oregon City. Even with the river crossing, Elias was confident that they could make those ten miles before dark.

Late in the afternoon, Elias could see a curl of smoke on the horizon in front of them. He rode forward until he could see that the smoke rose from a cabin's chimney.

Everything was open countryside, here. Massive pastures of rich farmland as far as the eye could see. Here and there, the grassland was dotted with stands of trees. But Elias had stopped worrying about trees. He'd had some moments, back on the wide open prairie where not a single tree could be seen on the horizon, that he worried he'd been taken. He worried he was coming to be a timberman in a country devoid of trees. But those fears were gone. In a thousand years he wouldn't run out of trees on the sides of Mount Hood. Not in a million years.

Not unless these boys working for him could start swinging their axes a lot faster.

Even this little cabin he was approaching stood under a black cottonwood.

There was a man in the yard picking squash. He had a bit of cultivated land, but he'd already harvested whatever he had growing there. The squash came from a little kitchen garden beside the cabin. He probably had two dozen or more head of cattle out behind the cabin. Elias figured he'd been in this cabin at least a year.

"How far to Oregon City, friend?" Elias said.

The man dropped his squash in a basket and came out walking toward the road. Here it was just tracks in the tall grass. "Y'all are coming in late in the year."

"Yes, sir," Elias said. "We didn't have the easiest time of it."

The man chuckled.

"You took Sam Barlow's road," he said. "You're the fourth or fifth wagon train come that road this year. You know what all the others said?"

Elias shook his head.

"I don't."

"They said they didn't have the easiest time of it. I heard Sam Barlow got out of town when folks started showing up looking for his head."

"Probably the smartest thing he's ever done," Elias said with a grin. "We can blame only some of our troubles on Mr. Barlow, and since he's a fellow Kentuckian, I'm willing to not go hunting for him."

"Mighty generous of you," the man said.

"I probably wouldn't have been quite as generous a few days back," Elias admitted.

"Well, you've almost made it. Oregon City is just four miles down the road. Keep going until you strike the Clackamas River. Follow the Clackamas to the south to the confluence with the Willamette River. There you'll find Oregon City, territorial capital."

Elias glanced to the south.

"We've been seeing smoke on the horizon all day," Elias said. He could see it now, sitting in his saddle. "What's that from?"

The man shook his head.

"Damn Injuns. They burn the Willamette Valley every damn summer when they move to their winter camps."

"For what purpose?" Elias asked.

"You tell me. I'm told they've been doing it since the beginning of time. The government's going to have to put a stop to it or we will," the man said.

"Is there any danger?" Elias asked.

The man shook his head.

"It usually burns itself out before it gets this far."

"How long have you been here?" Elias asked.

"This is my third year at this spot. But I been out in this country since ten years ago."

The man looked at the approaching wagons.

"You're welcome, if you like, to make your camp here tonight," he said. "Come into Oregon City nice and early tomorrow so there's plenty of time for all in your party to begin settling their affairs."

Elias nodded.

"That's kind of you," he said. "I think we'll do that."

RELIEF.

"No more river crossing," Jeff Pilcher said, holding his glass in the air.

"Praise the Lord!" Wiser McKinney said, taking a drink from his.

"No more mountains!" Captain Walker said.

"Praise the Lord!" Wiser McKinney laughed, and he took a drink.

"No more Laurel Hill!" Solomon McKinney said.

And every man in the company shouted "Praise the Lord!" and took a drink.

"To friends," Wiser McKinney said. "Elias Townes! Come have this drink with us. To friends!"

Whether it was the group of men drinking toasts to friendship, or a family huddled together talking about what they must do when they reached Oregon City to prepare for the coming winter or a man and wife turning in early because they were exhausted, or a single pregnant mother sitting alone at a campfire and mourning all she'd lost – relief swept through the Townes Party that night.

Other emotions fell around the camp, too. Grief. Trepidation. Excitement.

"After almost eight months together on this trail, it's hard to imagine that in just a few hours we'll be going our separate ways," Jefferson Pilcher said.

"We'll stay in touch with each other," Captain Walker said. "Any of you will be welcome in my home as long as the Lord sees fit to keep me on this side of the dirt."

Feeling his liquor, Captain Walker shouted his message at the rest of the wagon train.

"You hear that? You're all welcome in my home!"

In the morning, the wagon train started to break up.

Marcus Weiss and his family left first. They didn't even take time to make breakfast.

Jeb Smith sought out Elias and made an apology for the trouble he caused. The two men shook hands, and then Smith and his family started west for Oregon City.

Luke and Jacob Suttle set out with the Browns.

A few minutes later, Al Norton made a fast apology to Elias.

"I'd intended to go on to Oregon City with you," he said. "But my son Joshua, he wants to stay close to the Browns. You understand, I suppose, with a daughter who's married."

"I understand," Elias said. "Best wishes to you, Mr. Norton."

"And to you. I hope our paths cross again soon."

Jerry Bennett tried to see to it that people took only the livestock they were due, though here and there he might have let a steer go with the wrong family. It was hard to keep track, considering that some were lost on the way and others were butchered. But he was careful about the horses.

The McKinney brothers, both of them suffering headaches, also decided to go on to Oregon City. Sophie Bloom went with them, now driving her own wagon. Jefferson Pilcher spoke to Zeke Townes for quite a while that morning. The two had been side-by-side through much of the journey.

"I feel like I owe my life – and the lives of my family – to you, Zeke," Pilcher said. "I hope Oregon Territory ain't so big that we can't continue our acquaintance."

"I'm sure it's not, Jeff," Zeke said.

Pilcher hurried to try to catch up to the McKinney brothers, and Zeke sought out Elias.

"Shouldn't we get this wagon train moving?" Zeke asked.

"I'd rather not," Elias said. "I'd like to make our goodbyes here. I don't know why, but I feel like this is the end of a thing. Right now, this morning. And when we get into Oregon City, that's going to be the beginning of another thing. I won't want to waste time with goodbyes when I'm starting something new. We need to find this man Dodge who owns the land we're leasing and get up there."

Zeke chuckled.

"No rest for the wicked," he said.

Elias shrugged.

"The wagons are loaded. We won't need to buy much in the way of provisions in Oregon City. Let's go and find Dodge and then let's go find the land. That's how I see it."

"So, are we just going to wait for everyone else to leave?" Zeke said.

"We won't have to wait long," Elias said.

Even as he said it, Captain Walker came to say his farewells.

Stephen Barnes and his family started their wagon moving. The Grant family left behind him. Then John and Beth Gordon started to move. Within the hour, the only members of the Townes Party who remained were those who would be going on with the Townes brothers.

Then, at last, Zeke climbed into Duke's saddle, whistled at Towser and Mustard, and what remained of the Townes Party started the last four miles to Oregon City.

THE TOWNES BROTHERS SETTLED on the north facing side of a tall hill in the foothills of the Cascade Mountains. They liked this spot best because of its view of Mount Hood. Whatever memories that view inspired, fond or tragic, all of them knew that they'd done their best when they had to conquer that mountain.

That first winter they built three cabins and a bunkhouse with trees they cut on the spot. Elias and Madeline lived in one of the cabins with their sons and daughters, except for Maggie who lived with Jason in another cabin. Zeke and Marie and Daniel lived in the third cabin.

The hired men lived in the bunkhouse. Hugh Anderson, who sought Elias out in Oregon City, was the second new man Elias hired. Henry Blair was the first.

When the cabins were built, they constructed a sawmill down on the banks of the Clackamas River.

By the spring, they were cutting trees and floating them down the river to the sawmill. They floated their cut boards to Oregon City in small barges down the Clackamas River.

Every morning when she looked out her front door, Marie Townes could see Mount Hood towering in the distance.

She would always remember that first year as a lonely time. Zeke worked from sunup to sundown. Madeline was there, of course, and Maggie, and the younger girls, Martha and Mary. They helped with Daniel and they made a garden in the spring, and the days were pleasant. She had Towser and Mustard to keep her company on the front porch when Zeke worked late and Daniel went to bed. But when she thought of it in later years, she only remembered how lonely she was at the timber camp in the foothills of the Cascades.

"I think it's because I miss the wagon train," she told Zeke one night when they were talking and she confessed to him that she felt lonely. "Those people truly became like family. Even the ones I didn't care for. Well, most of them. We were all so close. We shared so much together. You know, Zeke, that's probably the biggest thing I'll ever do in my life. Traveling so far like that. It's a thing most people will never do. If you told me the whole wagon train was moving up here with us, I think I'd be delighted."

"Well, most of them," Zeke said.

But his mind was on his business, and he didn't have time to be lonely.

She wasn't wrong, he knew. None of them would probably ever do anything so enormous again in their lives. But it was done, and Zeke was ready to move on to the next thing.

Madeline, though, commiserated with Marie where her husband wouldn't.

"I feel lonely, too," she admitted. "We were surrounded by so long with so many people. There were always little children around. To tell the truth, I even miss Beth Gordon's gossiping. I feel like I want to know what's happening with everyone."

The next year, one of Jeb Smith's sons came and worked for Elias at the sawmill for a season.

Two years after that, Al Norton brought his youngest boy to see Elias. The boy started working for Elias and stayed on for three years. Norton spent about a week visiting with the Townes family, and they learned that Joshua Norton did marry Marianne Brown a few months after both families had gotten settled in Oregon City.

Shortly after Al Norton's visit, Elias and Madeline spent two weeks with Wiser McKinney.

The McKinney brothers had neighboring farms down in the valley. Betty Carlisle, Solomon's mother-in-law and Sophie Bloom's mother, had passed on by then. Sophie had met and married a man in Oregon City who owned a mercantile store and did a good business there.

They kept in touch, some of them. Their paths sometimes crossed.

Zeke had been in Oregon City on business one day when he ran into Captain Walker in a hotel saloon. Captain Walker had reenlisted and had recently returned from a campaign in the Cayuse war.

During that conversation, Zeke learned that Marcus Weiss started the hotel where they were drinking. But he'd died a year or two back, and Luisa and the two surviving children had sold the hotel and taken a ship back east.

"Is she happy there?" Zeke asked.

"I wouldn't know," Captain Walker said. "I heard that bit of news from John and Beth Gordon when I ran into them a few months back."

But they were intrepid people, all of them. And when Zeke or Elias or Marie or Maddie ran into someone or received a letter or paid a visit, they were never surprised to learn that those families who came west with them prospered. And without fail, on these encounters, those members of the wagon train always felt compelled to say a word of thanks to Elias Townes for seeing them to the Northwest Territory.

26

On July 3, 1923, Luther stepped off the train and held out a hand for his wife Nellie. She took his hand and carefully made the step down.

"Thank you," she said and patted his hand with her free hand before letting him go.

Luther took a big breath through his nose. The air smelled of coal from the train, but that didn't stop Luther from saying, "Smell that fresh, mountain air. Isn't it glorious?"

His younger son, Charles, who had just turned thirteen and was in an awkward phase between childhood and teenager, hopped down from the train, skipping the iron steps. His oldest boy, sixteen-year-old George, stepped down from the train and frowned at his younger brother. George frowned a lot these days. He was in a more awkward phase.

"Smell the air, George?"

"It smells like a train station," George said.

Luther laughed.

"A train station in the glorious Blue Mountains," he teased. Nothing was going to spoil this for him, not even a surly teenager.

They walked down the platform a ways until they came around the side of the depot, and Nellie actually gasped.

"Look at all the people," she said. Before her, filling the streets of this tiny mountain town of just fifty some odd residents, stood in eager anticipation a crowd of something close to twenty-thousand people. They were packed in the streets. Almost shoulder to shoulder. Here and there were men on horses. A few were dressed in ridiculous outfits, caricatures of the old emigrants.

Luther shook his head in amazement. He pushed his white, straw boater hat onto his head and gave the brim a little snap. He checked his watch. Their train had arrived right on time. It was exactly eight o'clock in the morning.

"President Harding's train is supposed to be here in an hour," Luther said. "Dad said that they were building an old Western town here especially for this occasion. Dad asked us to meet him there. Then we'll come back to see the president arrive."

"What did you say is the name of this town?" Nellie asked.

"Meacham," Luther said. "The old Oregon Trail cut right through here."

The family worked their way through the crowds of people.

"Boys, keep your eyes on your father so that you don't lose us," Nellie said. "With all these people here, I'm afraid we'd never find you if we got separated."

Luther Townes was a big man, tall and muscular. It was trait that ran in his family. It also wasn't difficult for him to make a way through the crowd. People tended to step out of his way.

"The flagpole there," George said. "Is that the town you're talking about?"

Luther looked the direction his son was pointing and saw the tall flagpole with an American flag flying over an enormous canvas tent. In front of the tent was a false-front of what was supposed to look like several log

223

cabins standing one next to the other. Each false front bore painted signs on the front. OK Bath House, one said. Another claimed to be a dance hall. Another read, Big Casino Gambling.

"I guess it's supposed to look like an old log fort," Luther said, and his wife sensed a drop in his enthusiasm.

The replica Western town had turned out to be no different from the men in their ridiculous costumes – just a caricature.

"Was there really a fort here?" Charlie asked.

They'd come some distance from the large crowd outside the train depot, but Luther had stopped walking and Nellie could see that he was disappointed by the lack of anything authentic. But this his eyes lit.

"There they are," Luther said. "My dad and Grandpa Gabe."

They were easy to spot from a distance. Luther's father, Cody Townes, was still an imposing figure at sixty-nine years old. He was a little hunched in the shoulders, but he stood tall. His arms rested on the back of the wheelchair. The man in the wheelchair wasn't nearly the imposing figure he had been when Luther was young.

Cody Townes stepped forward and shook his son's hand.

"I'm glad you made it. And glad you brought the boys," Cody said. He gave each of the boys a clap on the shoulder and a hug to his daughter-in-law.

"Grandpa Gabe," Luther said, speaking in a loud voice. "How was your trip here?"

"What's that?" the old man said. "At ninety-three, I don't hear so good anymore."

"I said how was your trip?" Luther asked again, louder this time.

Gabriel Townes laughed. He looked at his two great-grandsons.

"It's easier to get here by train than it is by wagon," he said with a laugh.

They'd come the night before. One of the organizations that invited President Harding to Meacham intended to honor anyone who was still alive who came across the Oregon Trail before 1853. Part of the festivities was a dinner the previous night, held inside the tent behind the false-front Western fort, to which those old-timers were invited.

"I was just telling your father, Luther, it was right here somewhere that we got lost."

Luther nodded his head and gave a glance at his father.

"Did you get lost last night, Dad?"

But Cody Townes shook his head. He'd heard the story plenty of times.

"The wagon train, Luther. We're talking about 1846 now."

"It's all changed," Gabriel Townes said. "This was all trees back then. Damn sure wasn't no town here. Or whatever that tent is supposed to be. But we're pretty near the spot where we lost our way. Ended up on an old Indian trail and had to cut our way out of the mountains."

"What do you mean cut?" Charlie asked.

"I mean we had to chop down the trees in our way. I had blisters like you wouldn't believe."

"You came all the way across the country in a wagon?" Charlie asked.

"All the way from Kentucky where our people are from," Gabe said. "I drove one of the wagons for my father and my uncle."

"How is mom?" Luther said to his father.

"Oh, she's fine. Glad she's not here today, I imagine. It's a hot one already."

"It was cold when we come through. Early snow that year," Gabriel said. He tugged on his son's sleeve. "Cody, I tried to tell your Aunt Mary that she should come to this, but she said she didn't feel up to it."

"That's what you said last night, Dad," Cody said. He turned back to Luther. "You're going to have to help me push this wheelchair through the grass if we're going back up to see the president's train."

"Oh, hell. I don't need this chair," Gabe said. "I can walk to see the president."

"Are you sure, Dad?" Cody said. "I don't want you to be too exhausted."

"Just push the thing up there so I can sit down while we wait for him. Damn train'll probably be late, anyway."

"Did you kill any Indians on the Oregon Trail?" Charlie asked.

Gabe chuckled a little. His eyes seemed to light with memories.

"Just the ones that needed it," he said.

"If he's going to walk, we'd probably better get started," Cody said.

Luther helped his grandfather from the wheelchair. George pushed it while Luther let Gabe hold onto his arm.

"Can you imagine all these people being here for this?" Luther said to his grandfather while they walked.

Gabe cast his eyes over the enormous crowd filling the tiny town of Meacham.

"I don't know what all the fuss is about, honestly. All we did was drive a wagon from one place to another."

Luther laughed.

"You opened up the Pacific Northwest. You settled all this land. Look at all the Townes family accomplished, Grandpa Gabe. Why, I'd bet half the buildings in Portland were built with lumber from your dad's sawmill."

"My father and Uncle Zeke couldn't have done better if they'd struck gold," Gabe said. "My dad especially, he was a smart businessman. You know he was the captain of that wagon train?"

"I think you've told me that," Luther said.

They'd walked only a little ways when Gabe said he needed to sit down. Luther pushed his grandfather in the wheelchair through the grass with George helping. Gabriel didn't argue with them.

Harding's train arrived on time, or close enough to it. He made a speech that almost no one could hear and then boarded a replica stagecoach that took him to a stage that was built for the occasion. The throngs of people followed him. Now, a man led the Townes family to a carriage. They helped Gabe in, and the family rode to the platform as well.

Luther helped his grandfather up to the platform, Gabe walking up the steps, and before the next round of speeches, President Harding recognized those present who had traveled the Emigrant Trail in 1853 or earlier. Gabe stood while the president spoke and shook the man's hand. President Harding said something that Gabe couldn't quite hear.

"I don't know what all the fuss is about," Gabe told the president. "The smart ones waited for the train to bring them."

Harding and some other people made speeches. Gabe dozed during the speeches.

Then the president, and the throngs, went to dedicate a rock and plaque erected to commemorate the Oregon Trail.

"I'm too hot and tired to keep following this man around," Gabe told his son. "And I've seen plenty of rocks."

They found a spot where they could catch a breeze under a big ponderosa pine with plenty of shade, and they rested there.

The old man seemed lost in his thoughts and didn't say anything for a while.

"Grandpa Gabe, I guess being here must bring back some memories," Luther said, hoping the old man might share a story to entertain the boys.

"Lots of memories," Gabriel said. "Eight months it took us to make the overland journey. We didn't have to seek our troubles. But you know what, doing that with my brother and sisters, my Uncle Zeke, and my own folks? I wish today it had taken us eight years. It was one of the best times of my life. I had a front row seat to see the man my father was, and that's a rare thing these days. I always after that had a lot of pride for my father. Proud when people said to me, 'Aren't you Elias Townes' son?' We had some rough dealings, not the least of which came from the very people who voted him to captain the wagon train. But he kept them together, mostly, and he got them all there. Most of them, anyway. I know he spent his life feeling bad about the ones that didn't make it."

"He was a good man," Cody agreed. "I have nothing but fond memories of him."

"They say there are ten graves for every mile of the Oregon Trail," Luther said, quoting something he'd read in the newspaper.

"That's not right," Gabe said. "There's graves they'll never know about."

THE END

Afterword

Dear Reader,

I want to thank you so much for joining me and the Townes Party on this Emigrant Trail journey.

I happily confess that I always have fun writing my novels. It is a thoroughly enjoyable experience for me, and there have been no exceptions to that. Some have been trying at times, and others don't come together as easily as I might prefer. But they're always fun.

And it's true, too, that I generally learn something new with every book. I do a tremendous amount of research before and during the writing of my novels. Some books require more research than others. Some books, whether through setting or time period, fall exactly inside my existing knowledge, and research is a simple refreshing. Others require me to delve deeper into the history books to expand my knowledge.

Though my novels are fiction, I do like for them to be accurate in terms of the setting and the time period. I hope, too, that readers can walk away from one of my books with their own knowledge expanded. I like to seek out and include those little-known historical details that make for a richer story. I'm certain that for at least some readers, these help to improve the reading experience.

I hope I was able to do that throughout this series. I know for myself, I learned a great deal about the Oregon Trail as I prepared to write this series.

Nevertheless, I'm going to confess to taking some liberties with history. Most of these liberties involved place names. I wanted the reader to be able to clearly follow along with the story, to know at least roughly where the characters were through each scene. To do this, I used modern names for places and landmarks.

For a number of specific reasons, I wanted to place the Townes Party on the Oregon Trail in 1846.

At that time, however, many of the named landmarks and places did not have commonly accepted names or had names that have changed over the years.

Massacre Rocks, for instance, was never called Massacre Rocks until 1852. Fort Kearney, mentioned in the first book, did not exist until 1848. But it helped me in the writing of this novel to conjure it into existence two years earlier because it served as a landmark to orient readers.

In this current novel and the previous one, I make mention of the Southern Route of the Snake River. In these books, I make the claim that it was non-existent, and in 1846, that was true. Eventually, emigrants did begin using the Southern Route to avoid crossing the Snake River. However, as the Townes Party discovered, water was difficult to come by because of the steep banks leading into the Snake River Canyon. But in the 1850s and 1860s, when the trail was tamer and more emigrants traveled across it, many definitely chose to make use of the Southern Route rather than attempt the dangerous crossings of the Snake River.

While historical accuracy was important to me, I fudged here and there for the sake of my narrative.

TRAGEDY ON THE BARLOW ROAD

In 1846, The Dalles wasn't a town. Instead, it was a mission, known as the Wascopam Mission, located on the banks of the Columbia River. The Dalles, a term in use by the Canadian fur trappers prior to 1846, specifically referred to the rapids between the now submerged Celilo Falls and the present site of the city.

In 1846, the Barlow Road – only constructed that spring – was officially the Mount Hood Road. I suspect that history recorded the route as the Barlow Road because it was commonly referred to that way in the late 1840s, but officially it was the Mount Hood Road.

I hope readers will understand and find these alterations to the historical record forgivable. In some of my other books, I've done the exact opposite: Sticking strictly to the historical record and utilizing outdated place names. But because the traveling is such an integral part of any story about the Oregon Trail, and because I didn't want to force readers who might choose to look up additional information to have to search too deeply to find what they were looking for, more often than not in this series I opted to use modern names to locate landmarks.

Another issue that confounded my writing is water flow in some of the mentioned rivers.

All of the big rivers, but especially the Columbia and the Snake, have been dammed since 1846. These dams have dramatically changed the way the rivers flow. Today some of these are relatively slow, meandering rivers, now easily navigated behind their dams. But they were once much more dangerous and fast flowing rivers. The Raft River, mentioned in the second book of this series, is hardly more than a wet spot now until it finally meets the Snake River. But source documents from those who actually traveled the Oregon Trail tell us that in the mid-1800s, the Raft River was often backed up by beaver dams and created a vast pool for travelers to cross. I described this in "To the Green Valleys Yonder," but anyone familiar with the current state of the Raft River might read my description of the story and wonder if I even know what water is, much less what the Raft River looks like.

I did my best to weigh all this out and tried to always err on the side of improving the experience for readers.

But I also understand that some readers who prefer strict historical accuracy might grumble. I understand, and can sympathize, with anger at my 1846 reference to the non-existent Fort Kearney or my reckless disregard for Wascopam Mission.

I took a few minor liberties with places and distance on the Barlow Road. In some cases, I stretched the distances, or shrank them, for the benefit of the narrative. But I tried to provide a fairly accurate depiction of the route the road took (accepting that in some places, we don't know today the actual route) and give readers a view of some of the highlights of the road.

I also managed somehow to lift an entire meadow and move it several miles west.

However, in researching the Barlow Road for this book, I came across some fascinating diaries from some of the men who were with Barlow either during his abandoned 1845 attempt to find a south route around Mount Hood or during his 1846 road building operation. I also consulted diary entries from several emigrants who took the Barlow Road in the mid-1800s.

Those who came on the trail in the late 1850s or after had a better time of it. The Trail from beginning to end was far more tame by then.

But those who cut their own trail, as Barlow did, committed truly heroic and almost unimaginable feats.

I think specifically of Joel Palmer who was with Barlow in 1845.

Reaching the summit above the White River, the men had no concept of where to go next or how to get there. In fact, below the summit was as far as their wagons would reach. The camp where they left their supplies for the winter (known by them as Fort Deposit) was there below the summit.

Palmer and two others decided to scale the bare, glacial side of Mount Hood, hoping to get a look at the landscape and find a route.

Writing in his own journal about the ascent on the side of Mount Hood, Palmer reports that he scaled the side of a glacial cliff, cutting handholds for himself as he went. He reached a high ledge where he was able to get a view of the terrain below him. But what I found fascinating was this bit of information: Palmer made this climb with "my moccasins ... worn out, and the soles of my feet exposed to the snow."

Imagine cutting your way through a thick Oregon forest and scaling the side of one of the High Cascades all with holes in your shoes!

Throughout the writing of this trilogy, I consulted primary sources wherever I could. Journals, diaries, memoirs. At every turn I found myself impressed by the hardy nature of the people who ventured off into the unknown West with only what their wagon could hold and what their oxen or mules could pull. And out of respect for those people, I tried to offer an accurate depiction of the Oregon Trail, even if the narrative sometimes required me to nudge the trail or the historical record a bit to fit my story.

I hope in the reading you were not too much annoyed by my intentional historical alterations.

Sincerely,

Robert Peecher

ALSO BY

If you enjoy Western series, I hope you'll check out my Heck & Early series, beginning with "Bred in the Bone."

Hector Espinosa and Early Bascomb are a couple of down-and-out saddle tramps, always looking for the next opportunity to earn a dollar. More often than not, the jobs they take require them to earn their keep behind a six-shooter.

If you enjoy fast-paced, gritty Westerns, the Heck & Early series is sure to be an instant favorite!

Grab a copy from Amazon today!

ALSO BY

If you enjoy crime thrillers, I'd be grateful if you would check out my Barnett Lowery series beginning with "Under the Dixie Moon."

It's deep-fried Southern justice when an investigator returns to his small town roots to take on a corrupt sheriff and the Dixie Mafia. If you love stories of down-home murder up in the hills of Dixie, small-town criminals, and deep-fried Southern justice, then slide into the passenger seat of this '67 Camaro and buckle up. You might want to bring along your Colt Python, because what gets buried Under the Dixie Moon always comes back up.

Click here to grab a copy today!

ABOUT THE AUTHOR

Robert Peecher is the author of more than 60 Westerns and crime novels. He's an avid outdoorsman and loves paddling rivers and hiking trails. He lives in Georgia with his wife Jean and a small kennel of dogs. You can follow him on Facebook at Robert Peecher Author.

Made in United States
Troutdale, OR
11/24/2024